STRIKE POINT

ADRIFT

EMERSON HAWK

Copyright © 2016 by Emerson Hawk

All rights reserved.

No part of this book may be reproduced in any form or by any electronic or mechanical means, including information storage and retrieval systems, without written permission from the author, except for the use of brief quotations in a book review.

FOREWORD

This is fiction.
Fiction is make believe.
Even if something may appear to be set in the real world, it is still pretend.
Some of the things you read in this novel will make sense in the real world.
Other things won't. That's where we pretend.

* * *

If you find that you really like this story, please let others know by leaving a good review.

CHAPTER 1

I wasn't sure how many days or weeks it had been since the EMPs. Hell, it could've been months by now.

From the time the train stopped on the tracks and the tornadoes started, to us meeting Ben in his barn outside of Tipton, we'd lost all track of time. The EMPs took out all electronics, and after a few days, we were more concerned about survival than what time or what day it was. The days and nights had begun to run together as we worked with Ben to secure his property and we'd become like a family. We knew we would always be welcome there and that was comforting, since we had no way of knowing what lay in store for us as we got closer to St. Louis.

We'd managed to make our way into Jefferson City. After a few close calls, and Lisa killing the owner of the boat we were on, we were finally headed home.

The gentle motion of the boat was relaxing which was a nice change from the previous day. We'd tried to find a place to bury the boat owner, but the best we could do under the circumstances was to leave him under a tree. We did not have the tools or the time to dig a grave. Hell, from what we'd seen, most people were just burning bodies in big piles.

Lisa was having difficulty dealing with the trauma of having shot someone. David was doing his best to comfort her and I could tell he was concerned about her well-being. He had fallen hard for her, even though he had not professed his love. But a guy knows.

I could tell he wanted to protect her and make sure that she was okay. I'm sure he hated the fact that she'd felt it was necessary to take a man's life. She'd probably thought that if we didn't get the boat that we might've died trying to make it home. I can only imagine that in her mind she must have thought it was a life or death situation.

Laura and I both sat in silence as we thought about all of the things that had happened in the last several weeks. Our good fortune in meeting Ben and George, and how without them, we'd most likely still be stuck in the FEMA camp under the thumb of the maniac, Kron.

Ben was such a good man, so kind and generous. It was nice to know that there were still people who cared about others and were willing to share what they had. In return we'd made sure to leave him in a good position to continue surviving with as little effort as possible.

I thought about George and I hoped he'd made it back to Tipton without incident. That sweet 66 Mustang would have been a nice way to show up in St. Louis, but General Knox made it clear that it was not a wise choice to take a car. Especially, because we were not skilled at fighting against larger groups of people. It could have been deadly.

As we floated down the river, I noticed several people would appear randomly along the shoreline; gathering water or trying to catch fish. Some people looked like zombies. Others looked quite well fed. I imagined that those that were well fed had been used to living in the country and knew how to forage and trap food for themselves. Or they were probably preppers that had their own food storage.

A few years back, Laura had decided that it'd be a good idea to begin storing food. She had read that we needed to have a year's worth of food stored in case of an emergency, and I hadn't seen any harm in doing so.

At first, it was fine, but we weren't using all the food she was buying before it would expire.

I was always afraid to eat food that had been past the expiration date. Laura was much more lenient when it came to expiration dates. She felt that if she opened up the can and it didn't smell or taste rancid that it would most likely be safe, even if it was a couple of years old. I was never quite convinced, and wound up throwing away a lot of food that had gone way past its expiration date.

I began to grow weary of hearing that there was going to be an economic collapse, a pandemic or earthquake that never came. And while I didn't believe most of what the mainstream media said, the alternative news seemed to constantly be in a state that the worst was just around the corner. So after a few years, we both decided that it was a waste of money to have that much food stored and began to downsize it a bit.

Eventually, we stopped preparing altogether after life continued without anything major happening to change what we saw as normal.

Considering we were not at home when the EMP disaster struck, all that preparation wouldn't have made a damn bit of difference. I mean, even if we had prepped for a year's worth of food, it wouldn't have helped us when the train had stopped and we were 150 miles outside of

STRIKE POINT: ADRIFT

St. Louis.

In fact, what would have served us better is if we had studied just what plants were edible and how to trap food and find water that was drinkable. If we had not met Ben, we might have been dead already. I was glad George and David were able to teach me a few things that I could use in the future.

I was also glad that Benjamin had stored some food. Growing up during the depression, his family had lived through harder times. He'd known the value of stored canned goods and meats when times were tough and food was scarce. What Ben had been able to teach us in the short time we'd been there would give us a good head start, due to the skills we now possessed.

Laura reached over and gave my hand a squeeze as I found myself daydreaming about a fresh start. Between the stress and anxiety of the day before, it was nice to allow myself a moment to dream. That moment was cut short by David's voice.

"I think we have a problem."

My heart began racing as I stood up and looked to where he was pointing. The sky was turning black once again.

CHAPTER 2

"I'd hoped we were done with these damn storms!" John said as he abruptly stood up and turned the engine key.

Panic began to set in as he frantically tried to turn the engine over, but it was out of gas. John slammed his fist on the dash as they watched the dark clouds billow towards them with ever increasing speed.

The wind began to push the boat violently back and forth on the water, as they heard the trees groaning and crackling.

"We have to get off this river! If that storm hits us there's no telling where we'll end up," David yelled.

"You girls get down below and hold onto something. This may be a bumpy ride," John yelled.

Laura and Lisa scrambled down into the front of the boat and grabbed onto the rails as they watched from below. It wasn't a large boat and only had a small front area for someone to sleep if needed and it was full of junk that used to belong to the boat guy.

STRIKE POINT: ADRIFT

John relentlessly turned the key in the hope that the engine would find some life.

"I think we might be out of fuel. But I don't know how to tell. The gas gauge has not been above the empty even after we put the gallon or so in it," John said.

David tried to keep his oar in the water to use as a rudder as the winds began to turn the boat and before they knew it, they were being spun in a circle on the water like a child's toy, caught up in a whirlpool in the tub as the water drained out.

David and John held on for dear life as the boat spun around and around, causing them to become dizzy and nauseated.

Thunder boomed and both girls let out a yelp as the wind forced the boat to its will.

They watched as the sky began to roll with dark heavy clouds. A spider web of lightning reached out from under the clouds and struck a tree on the shoreline, causing it to crack and fall into the river.

"Hang on!" David yelled to everyone as the boat stopped spinning from one direction and began to spin the other direction. It was like being on some kind of bad carnival ride that everyone wanted off of.

Sideways rain slapped John's face and hands, stinging like a hundred ant bites all at once. He tried to cover his face with his arm and shirt but the rain just was relentless.

John and David watched helplessly as the boat spun towards the shore.

"Hang on tight! We're going to hit the shore!" David yelled out.

It was if the devil himself had picked them up and tossed them in between a fallen group of trees and the shoreline. They came to a stop as the wind continued to pound them. David wanted to try to tie them off to something, but he was afraid to let go of the rails for fear he'd be thrown into the river and drowned.

What'd seemed like hours was only minutes, before the storm passed as quickly as it had come.

"Are you okay?" John yelled down to the girls.

"Yes, we're fine," Laura said as she and Lisa came up from below, soaked from the rain that had poured down on them from above.

Lisa rushed over to David to give him a hug as he pulled her into him and let her know that everything was okay. Laura and John held each other tight, grateful that none of them had gotten hurt.

"I thought these storms were over. This was almost as bad as that first tornado at the train," Laura said in a shaky voice.

After taking a few minutes to calm down, they evaluated their situation. As if things couldn't get any worse, the boat was tightly wedged between some downed trees and a sand bar.

"Well, looks like we're all going for a swim," David said with a heavy sigh.

CHAPTER 3

"This boat is wedged in tight. With the way the current is pushing at it, it'll be a pain to try to get it out," David said.

I looked at him and shook my head, not knowing exactly what to do either. We were wedged in such a way that the only way to get to shore was to get in the water, and we had no idea how deep it was at that point. The water was moving pretty swiftly and I was concerned that we might have a problem with getting swept away.

"Laura, how many life jackets did you see down there?" I asked.

"I think I only saw two, let me go check," she said, descending back down into the front of the boat. She came up with two life jackets and laid them on the floor.

"This is all I could find. Although I think the bench seat cushions might float."

"No, that won't work. Trying to use the seat cushions as a life jacket would actually be more dangerous than using nothing," David replied. "I think the girls should use the life jackets and we'll just tie some rope around us to keep from being pulled away."

David and I tied ourselves off to a couple of trees and made sure the girls' life jackets were secure. Then, David and I got into the water to try and lift the back of the boat up enough to free it.

The shock of the cold water surprised me. Even though it was probably mid-May, the river felt like it was an ice bath. I began to shiver almost immediately.

We first tried to move the boat with just David and I in the water, and the girls used the two oars to try to push off from the trees.

The boat was caught firmly. We had to eliminate any extra weight, in order to lift it enough to budge it.

The girls got into the water and up in front of the boat where they would be safer from the river currents and not be pulled under. The undercurrent was swift and at least if it caught David or I, we'd be tied up and wouldn't be swept away.

David and I managed to find a place at the back of the boat and as we counted to three, all of us tried to lift the boat up and push it off the sandbar. It was moving, but the tail end was still too low for us to get it off the sand bar.

"Why don't Lisa and I get on the top front of the boat where it's wedged under the tree, and push down while you guys lift the back?" Laura suggested.

David nodded and the girls made their way to the front of the boat and used their backs and legs to push against the tree, pushing down on the front of the boat. After the third push, the boat sprang free and allowed us to grab it, but when the boat released it caught Laura off guard and she flipped back over the tree and into the

STRIKE POINT: ADRIFT

river.

"John! Help!" Laura yelled as she began to helplessly float downstream.

"Hang on! I'm coming!" I yelled as I instinctually swam towards her to try to catch her without thinking. As I made my way into the depths of the river, the undercurrent kept trying to pull me downward. My arms burned as I pushed as hard as I could. Even though I was going downstream, I was fighting the undercurrent from pulling me under.

"Swim sideways to the shore!" I yelled as I began to get closer to her. Just as I was about to reach her, I was abruptly stopped by the rope around my waist.

"Dammit!" I yelled as I realized I had forgotten about the rope when I'd begun to swim after her.

Laura managed to grab onto a old dock pole that was sticking out into the river, holding on for dear life.

"Hang on, babe!" I yelled as I swam sideways towards the shore. As soon as I hit land, David untied the rope and ran towards me, quickly tying it off again so I could get back out to her.

Exhausted already, I swam towards her and barely reached her before the current tried pulling me away. My fingertips brushed one of the straps on her life jacket and I was able to hook it just before the current pushed me too far.

"Let go, babe. I've got you," I said as she felt me tug and let go of the pole, both of us kicking hard towards the shore.

We finally made it to the shore and collapsed in a heap of exhausted flesh.

"Next time you decide that you want to go for a swim, let's go to a lake instead of the river," I said with a nervous laugh as I tried to catch my breath. My emotions were a tangle of relief, fear and joy that neither one of us had died today.

Lisa and David came running to make sure we were okay. "I thought we'd lost you. I'm glad you held on," David said.

Shivering from the ice cold water and from almost losing Laura, I nodded as I turned to face her.

"You okay?" I asked.

She nodded, her lips quivering as her eyes began to tear up. I knew she was scared. I was scared too. I didn't want to lose her. Ever.

Bringing myself upright on wobbly legs, I helped Laura to her feet. We were all soaking wet, but the boat had been freed and we were all still alive.

I looked across the adjacent field and noticed several cows.

"Looks like we had an audience," Laura said with a ragged laugh as she pointed to the cows watching us, looking bored. We all laughed a little at the sight of it.

"Yeah, but there's something even better that I see. Look over there," David said and he pointed to a run-in shed.

CHAPTER 4

We all made our way back to the boat, securing it for the night and gathered our bags. Making our way across the field, the cows didn't seem to mind our company as we headed into the shed.

"What is this thing?" Lisa asked.

We were standing inside a building that had one wall missing. The other three walls and the roof were solid.

"It's an open sided shed for livestock to stay under for shade or if they want to get out of the rain. Most of the time, cows don't care if they get wet, but in the heat of the summer, it can provide shade to keep them from overheating," David explained.

"Fortunately, it doesn't look like it has been used a lot lately. Probably because it hasn't really gotten that hot yet, or it would be full of cow patties," Laura joked.

"Do we have anything to build a fire?" I asked. We were all still shivering from being in the cold, wet clothes.

"Yes, I have a fire steel. I'll just need to dig a hole first,"

EMERSON HAWK

David replied.

"A hole? What for?" Lisa asked.

"It's called a Dakota fire pit. George showed me how to do it. It's designed to have a fire, but will keep the flames low so that it isn't as noticeable. I figure the last thing we want to do is draw attention to ourselves. And with no power, any kind of light will easily be seen," David replied.

It was a good idea. We needed to make sure that whatever we did would not attract unwanted attention. It was important that we kept ourselves hidden as much as possible. It was just too dangerous to be seen.

He opened up his backpack and took out a small folding Army shovel.

David dug a hole that was about a foot deep and about the size of a large dinner plate. He then checked the direction of the wind and began to dig an airway hole that was up wind of the bigger hole.

The airway hole was going to be about the size of his forearm from elbow to hand. He dug down and at an angle towards the bigger hole, meeting up at the bottom. Once completed it would feed the main fire hole with the air needed, acting like a bellows to keep the fire going.

He filled the main fire hole with some small brush and used his fire steel to create the spark needed to light the fire. Once the fire was lit the air would pull from the angled side hole and bring the oxygen into the fire pit to keep it lit for hours.

"That's pretty neat," Lisa said. She smiled sweetly at David as he continued to build up the fire.

"We need to gather a bunch of wood and sticks before it gets too dark to see," David said.

Everyone took off in different directions and we gathered up twigs, sticks and a few pieces of larger wood.

It didn't take long for everything to get nice and warm

STRIKE POINT: ADRIFT

underneath the shed. The light of the fire was in the hole but the heat filled the area nicely. We watched as the sun began to set and dug out some of the ham and potato soup that Lisa had managed to bring with her.

"How did you manage to get that to stay in your backpack without getting busted all over the place?" Laura asked.

"I took several zipper baggies and put them inside of each other, then filled the bag up with the soup and made sure to squeeze out as much air as possible. Then triple bagged it so that I could essentially roll it up and put it in my satchel," Lisa replied. "I wasn't sure it would work, but it did!"

"That's pretty smart thinking," David said with a sheepish grin.

Lisa pulled out a can of peaches that had one of those pop tops and pulled it open, giving each of us a few slices and shared the juice.

"I hate wet underwear," Laura said as she began to squirm in her wet jeans. Everyone let out a chuckle at the sudden change in conversation.

"Well, you can always take them off," I said to her with a wink and a smile.

She giggled and decided that she wanted to change into a dry pair. She dug through her backpack and found her other pair of pants, a pair of shorts and some dry underwear she'd put into zipper bags.

"I need to go change. Will you walk back over to the boat with me?" she asked.

"Sure, but all we really need to do is go to the other side of the shed. No one can see you out here. Except nosy cows," I laughed.

"Funny." Laura's sarcasm was thick as she rolled her eyes at me.

EMERSON HAWK

I decided to let Lisa and David have a few moments to themselves so I walked over to the boat with Laura, since it was beginning to get dark and we would eventually have no way to see without using a flashlight. I didn't want to use the flashlights because I was afraid we'd be noticed.

"Okay, but we need to hurry. It'll be too dark to see soon," I said, as we took her things over to the boat.

Laura hopped onto the boat and went down into the lower area under the front deck.

"I don't think you're going to want to be wearing shorts out here. You'll get eaten alive by mosquitoes and other biting bugs," I suggested.

"I don't know which would be worse. Having wet pants and underwear or being eaten alive by mosquitoes. It's a tossup," she joked.

I watched her from above as she stripped down and admired the view. She decided to go with a dry pair of pants instead. Smart choice.

As I looked over at where the fire pit was inside the shed, I could barely see it flickering just above the ground's surface. I thought that was pretty neat to have a fire but not have it be seen. That would come in handy later down the road if I ever needed it.

Laura brought her wet clothes up to hang in the shed, hoping to dry them out overnight.

"That's much better. I just couldn't deal with wet underwear. I don't know why it bothers me so much. But it just feels gross," Laura said.

"I get it. Plus, it was nice seeing you half naked," I giggled as I pulled her close to me and gave her a big hug.

"Do you think we'll make it back to St. Louis, okay?" Laura asked.

"I'm going to make sure that we get there safely. I really want to get home now. If it wasn't so hard to see in the

STRIKE POINT: ADRIFT

dark, I'd say let's get back on the river now. But it's just too dangerous not being able to see and not having any light," I said.

"I feel safer during the day anyway. If we'd been on the river and it was dark when that storm had hit, I don't know if we'd all still be here," Laura said.

"Agreed. Well, I hope the cows don't mind if we borrow their space," I said. Laura giggled as we walked back to the shed.

But by the time we got there, all we could hear was the sound of Lisa sobbing.

CHAPTER 5

As Laura and John made their way back to the shed, they heard Lisa sobbing uncontrollably.

"What happened?" John asked.

"I think it's finally hit her that she killed somebody. I think she's reliving it and trying to deal," David said, as he tried his best to comfort her.

Laura sat down next to Lisa and pushed her hair out of her face. "I can't imagine how you must feel. I know you did what you thought was right, and you were able to save us from having to walk. But I can't imagine that you feel any better about it. I'm sorry, honey."

Lisa couldn't say anything. She was shaking and trembling, as she sobbed harder and harder. It was like she was having some type of mental break.

John speculated that she just couldn't handle dealing with having killed someone. He worried that she would recoil when the time came for her to have to fight again, if she ever needed it.

STRIKE POINT: ADRIFT

David pulled Lisa into his shoulder and wrapped his arms around her, pulling her close and holding her tight. He leaned back against the wall of the shed and tried to warm her up. The fire was helping but it was slow, since David and Lisa were still wearing their wet clothes.

Then, David surprised all of them when he began to softly sing.

John and Laura sat quietly as the words to You've Got A Friend began to softly echo inside the shed.

Before long, Lisa began to calm down. He kept holding her and gently stroking her shoulder as she began to breathe slower and was able to get herself under control.

John and Laura leaned back against the wall as John put his arm around her and pulled her close. They sat quietly and let David continue singing to Lisa. Laura was intrigued by David's instinct to take this approach in trying to calm her.

Lisa finally stopped crying and just listened to the sound of David's soothing voice.

When he'd finished, Lisa looked up at David and gently kissed him on the lips. David reciprocated and pulled Lisa close to him as their kiss became much more passionate.

Laura and John tried to focus their attention on the fire. They didn't want to say or do anything to make the two feel awkward or out of place. After a few moments of passionate kissing, Lisa pulled back and looked deeply into David's eyes.

"Marry me," David said.

Lisa pushed herself up into a seated position. "What? What did you say?"

David sat up and faced her. "I love you, Lisa. I fell for you the day we met back at the prison camp. I knew as soon as I met you that you were the one for me. Marry me."

"But, how? Everything's different now. There's no records or judges or… I don't know…" Lisa stammered.

"All you have to say is 'yes,'" David asked again.

A soft smile shown on his young face as he reached up and brushed her hair out of her eyes, the back of his hand gently stroking her cheek.

"Yes, of course! Yes!" Lisa said as she reached out and grabbed him, kissing him again.

John and Laura were sitting back silently watching and grinning big, trying not to interfere with what was happening. It was such a special moment that they were glad to be a witnesses of it.

Lisa and David finally released each other and began to giggle like teenagers. It was new and unfamiliar to both of them and they weren't sure how to handle their emotions.

Laura couldn't contain herself any longer. "Congratulations!"

Lisa and David looked over at John and Laura and let out a loud laugh when they realized that they weren't alone once again. During their small interlude, they had shut out all parts of the world, except for just the two of them.

The sun had almost set and there was just a small amount of light left in the sky. They were finally drying out and John and David decided to try to set up a small fishing trap right on the edge of the river before it got too dark. John dug out his flashlight and it still had some battery life left, so John and David went down to the river's edge and set up a fishing trap with rocks and sticks.

John watched David as he created a half circle with

STRIKE POINT: ADRIFT

sticks and rocks, that curled around into its own center. He then took a large log and placed it sticking out from the side. It created a way for fish to be redirected into the trap but unable to get back out. John thought it was brilliant.

"George teach you that?" John asked.

"Actually, this was something my dad taught me before he died."

"Oh, I'm sorry," John said.

"It's okay. It was a long time ago."

"So, you're engaged now. How does it feel?" asked John.

"Like I can do anything. I feel like I'm on top of the world," David replied.

CHAPTER 6

"Well, I'll be darned." I was surprised to see there were three medium-sized fish stuck in the fish trap. I didn't actually think it would work, but it did. Now we just had to retrieve them and get them back to the shed. David found an old fishing net in one of the boat storage boxes and brought it out to put the fish in.

"Breakfast!" David said, as he held up the net to show the girls his catch.

I took the shovel and scooped out some of the dead charcoal pieces. I used the pieces to filter the water before I'd restock the fire that had gone down overnight. Finding a flat rock, David began gutting and scaling the fish.

"I think I saw a few more flat rocks near the water's edge. If you can bring them over, we can use them to cook on," David suggested.

Laura and I found two long, flat rocks that worked

STRIKE POINT: ADRIFT

perfectly to partially cover each side of the hole, still allowing much of the flame and heat to come through. We could use the stones to cook the fish, and to help heat up some river water in cans.

Our water supply had dwindled quite a bit. I decided to work on replenishing our water while David worked on the fish.

George had given me a small handkerchief before we had left. With that, I would need to do a small amount of water at a time, but he'd also explained how to filter water if I ever needed to do it out in the wild.

George had told me that by using sand, rocks, and charcoal, we could essentially filter water that would be safe enough to drink; once we boiled it to kill any microorganisms that we couldn't see.

The one thing that there seemed to be an endless supply of was used empty plastic bottles. After finding a few, I rinsed them and the leftover peaches can in the river. I cut the bottles in half, and took off the caps. I then flipped the top half of each upside down and pushed it into the bottom half of the bottle.

I used a few small pieces of my ripped t-shirt to act as the first layer. Then I filled it with a layer of sand, a layer of rock, and a layer of charcoal that I had rinsed as well. It took a few times before the water began to run clear. But once it did, I set up several more.

Lisa managed to find a couple more cans that just needed to be washed, and we began an assembly line of water filtering. I would dump the filtered water into the cans, and she would make sure the water came to a boil.

It was a long and tedious process, but I knew that we would need to have plenty of water if we were going to survive. Not having enough water in this environment was a deadly prospect. Even more so than not having

EMERSON HAWK

enough food.

It took several hours to finish cooking the fish and eating, also boiling the water and allowing it to cool down. The girls managed to find us a couple of other cans that we used to add more water to the fire pit so that it could boil as well. Once the water boiled, we took the hot can and just set it in the river submerged halfway to cool it down quickly without contaminating the boiled water. That helped to cut some of the time off of sanitization, but we still took more time making water than I'd really wanted to.

"Too bad we didn't find another well!" Lisa laughed, remembering back to the ice-cold water that had come out of Ben's well when we'd first stumbled on his barn.

We hydrated ourselves and filled up as many water bottles as we could find. We hoped that we'd be able to get water again when we needed it.

"We really need to find fuel. If we could get this thing full, we could be in St. Louis in two hours," David said.

"Yeah, I know, but it beats walking," I replied.

Even if we were just floating, it was still faster and less tedious than walking all the way back on the railroad tracks.

"So, we're going to try this again? Try floating and navigating using just the oars to hopefully get us to someplace where we can get fuel?" Laura asked.

"Yes, that's the plan. If I remember, there was some type of boat landing in Hermann and if we can get there, I think we might be able to find fuel. Or at least find some cars that we can steal the gas out of. We still have the gas cans, they just don't hold very much and I know this fuel tank needs a lot more than just a couple of gallons," I replied.

STRIKE POINT: ADRIFT

"I don't like the idea of being on the river and not being able to get away if someone comes up on us. It's risky," Laura said.

I looked at her quizzically. "Would you rather walk?"

She shook her head. "No, no I don't want to walk. It's risky if we walk and it's risky if we ride the river. I'd rather take my chances on the water."

We finished getting everything back into the boat and covering up any trace of where we'd stayed in the shed. We made sure to fill in the Dakota fire pit, so that no humans or animals would get injured by stepping in the hole or that the fire pit would catch something on fire after we'd left.

"Gonna be hot today," David said, as he used the oars to push us off the embankment.

We decided to stay as close to the edge of the river as possible and yet still stay within the current so we wouldn't hit any stumps or trees that might have fallen into the river.

David and Lisa sat at the back edge of the boat and slowly guided us into the current, keeping us going downstream.

The peace and quiet of the river made it easy to forget that where we were heading was going to be anything but peaceful.

CHAPTER 7

As the day went on, the heat began to rise, in more ways than one. David and Lisa sat at the back of the boat and spent most of their time staring longingly into each other's eyes. Looking at them, you'd have thought that the world was all good and that nothing bad had happened.

Laura and I tried to mind our own business as we kept watch on the shore and looked out for any other boaters.

"So, do you think there's still places to get married in the city? So that we can make it all legal and stuff?" Lisa asked David.

"I'm sure there's some way that we can make it legal. But even if we can't find a judge or a place to get married, we can still be married. There's nothing that says we can't commit to each other and be married. That's how they used to do it before the states got involved. People would just find a priest and a Bible and that's how

STRIKE POINT: ADRIFT

they would declare their love and commitment to each other," David replied.

We giggled at the newness of their love and how special it was, considering what was going on in the world.

It almost felt like we'd had a hand in bringing them together. If David hadn't been one of the guards at the prison that we'd escaped from, and Lisa had not survived the train being tossed by a tornado after the EMP, they wouldn't have met. Laura and I both agreed that it was the apocalypse that had brought them together. What a way to start a relationship.

Laura leaned into me and put her head on my shoulder as we stood at the front of the boat, watching the trees on the shore slowly pass us by.

"I remember when our love was new. It was so special and I was so lucky to have found you. I couldn't have asked for a better person to go through the apocalypse with," Laura's laugh sounded like she was trying to be happy, but I knew her too well. There was sadness in that laugh.

I wrapped my arm around her waist and pulled her into me. "Well, you're actually holding up quite well considering. Although, I hate to say it, but I have a feeling things are going to get quite a bit worse and may be a little harder to live with."

"What do you mean?" Laura asked.

"Well, we've been pretty sheltered from a lot of the really bad stuff. I mean, staying at Ben's has been a blessing in disguise. We've not had to figure out how to survive without help. When we went through Jefferson City, it was eye-opening to me. And I have a feeling that St. Louis is not going to be much better. In fact, it'll probably be much worse," I replied.

I don't think Laura completely understood just what

EMERSON HAWK

we were heading into. Hell, I really wasn't sure either. I knew it was going to be difficult, probably even more than I had imagined. I hoped that we weren't making the wrong decision by heading towards the city. It might have been a better option for us to have stayed back at Ben's house until some kind of new law and order was regained. Right now, under Martial Law, who knew what things were going to be like in the cities.

Thinking back to TV shows that speculated about the apocalypse or some major disaster, it always seemed that people would die off quickly because they weren't thinking clearly, from starvation and dehydration.

We had been well fed for quite some time, and hadn't really experienced much hunger. I knew that it was something we were going to become very familiar with in the upcoming weeks.

David and Lisa were clearly in their own little bubble, talking about wedding plans that might never happen. I knew that life would burst that bubble soon enough, so I let them be.

Laura went down below and found a can of corn that she brought up to open for lunch. "Before you open that, are you really hungry right now? Or are you eating just because it's close to lunchtime?"

Laura gave me a questioned look as if I were trying to trick her.

"I am kinda hungry. Not starving, but I could use something. I thought I would share with everyone, if that's okay. It's not like this is going to go very far, but it could keep our tummies from rumbling," she replied.

I bit my tongue as I nodded my head for her to go ahead and open the can of corn. Part of me felt like it would be a wise decision to hold off on eating until we were really hungry, but the other part of me thought that

STRIKE POINT: ADRIFT

it made sense to try to eat a little all along to keep from getting severely hungry. I wasn't sure which way would be best for us to function, but the idea of trying to make what little rations we had last was really important.

Laura grabbed a spoon, took several large spoonfuls and shoved them in her mouth, making sure to get some of the juice before handing it to me.

I took my two spoonfuls and handed the can to David and Lisa who finished it off. It wasn't a lot, but corn being a high starch vegetable and having some sugars, would help to stave off that gut gnawing hunger that would eventually come. We saved the can for boiling water later, if we needed to.

"I think we all need to think about the best way to make our food supply last as long as possible. We don't know how long it will be before we get another chance to replenish, and I don't want us to start fighting over food," I said to everyone.

David nodded his head as he half listened to my statement. His mind was completely wrapped up with Lisa at the moment.

I understood how love could take over the brain and make the body do things that it normally wouldn't do. Such as, forgo food because love is all you think you need. That could work to our advantage right now, but I still wanted to make sure that everyone was continuing to be fed enough.

I decided that I would wait and continue this conversation at another time, since no one seemed to be interested in having it. I knew eventually, there would come a time that we would have to talk about how we divided up our food supply and who got what.

I also knew that we needed to become more adept at trapping and snaring food. George had shown me sev-

EMERSON HAWK

eral things back at Ben's house, but we hadn't taken the time to put them into practice before we'd left. It would be one of those things that I would have to learn as we went.

Going through a checklist in my head, I turned my attention back to watching the river. As I looked up, I barely had enough time to get David's attention. There was someone in another boat, heading right for us.

CHAPTER 8

avid," John said, trying to wrestle David's attention from Lisa. "David!"

David finally responded and stood up quickly, noticing the two men in a small fishing boat approaching.

"Girls, go down below and get your rifles ready. Stay out of sight unless we start taking gunfire. We don't want anyone to know that you're here," David said.

Laura and Lisa quickly made their way down below and readied themselves behind the door, in case they needed to come out and help the guys.

David pulled the oar out from the back rig so that it wouldn't be obvious that they had no fuel. Still dressed in his military uniform, he wasn't sure if he would be welcomed or not.

"We want to act like everything is as normal as can be," David whispered to John. John acknowledged him as he flipped the safety off his rifle and pulled the strap up over his shoulder.

It became clear that these men were of foreign descent. They both wore the same kind of skullcap style hat with no markings. One was sitting in back holding the throttle on the outboard motor, the other was sitting on the front bench. Both had rifles across their laps.

"Howdy, how y'all doing?" The thick Arabic accent was immediately noticed, no matter how hard they tried to sound American.

"We're doing just fine," John replied curtly.

"Where you headed?" the second guy asked, with an even thicker accent.

"Why?" David asked, reaching back and palming the butt of his pistol.

The guy that was in front raised his hand up, as if to say 'just relax'. The other guy slowed the motor just enough to circle them.

"Just trying to be friendly. There's a lot of places these days that aren't very safe anymore," the front guy said.

"Y'all got any food?" the rear guy asked.

"Just enough for today. After that, we'll be SOL until we can find a place to get some more. Do you know of a place where we can resupply?" John asked, putting the questions back to them.

The guy in the front of the boat looked back towards the guy in the back and gave him a slight grin. "I believe there is a camp down in Hermann where they're giving food and water to anyone who needs it."

"A camp? What kind of camp?" David asked.

The fishing boat continued to slowly circle, making both of them uncomfortable, but they stayed calm since both of the men in the other boat were not acting in any kind of threatening way.

STRIKE POINT: ADRIFT

"It's a FEMA camp. You'll see it right past the bridge. But you'll have to give up your boat and your freedom, if you want some of their food," the guy said.

The glance John gave to David said he figured it was similar to what had happened back at the prison in Tipton. Unfortunately, they were out of options. They were running out of food, and they needed fuel for the boat.

"You never did say where you were heading," the front guy asked.

"We're heading to St. Louis," John said. He figured that it was a pretty big city and it really didn't matter if these two knew anyway.

"Oh… St. Louis. Okay, have you been there since the blackout?" the front guy asked.

David and John shook their heads.

"Well, you're in for a big surprise. St. Louis is not what it used to be. It's pretty crazy there now. If you're planning on heading there, I suggest you go well armed and plan on hiding a lot," he said.

"Hiding a lot?" David replied.

"Uh-huh. There's a lot of things that have been taken over now. It's really dangerous in the city. If you're not part of a gang, then you are considered an enemy. And if you want to be part of the gang, you have to steal and kill to be protected. It's really bad. We managed to escape and decided to stay away from the city," the guy explained.

John and David were beginning to think that these guys weren't all that bad. They seemed just like anyone else who may have been searching for food and protecting themselves from others.

"Do you guys need a tow?" the rear guy asked.

David quickly spoke up. "No, thank you. We're just taking a break to see how the fish are biting. We were hoping to find a spot to get some good catfish or crappie," David said.

The first guy studied John and David quite hard before responding.

"That's gonna be kinda hard without any fishing poles," the other guy joked.

"We have other ways to catch fish. We just have to find the right spot." David said as he pulled out a hand grenade from his lower leg pocket.

Both men raised an eyebrow once David showed the hand grenade to them. It was obviously unexpected, and even John was a little surprised.

"Well, you guys take care and we wish you the best of luck. I hope your new fishing technique works well for you," they said before revving their engine and taking off back down river.

John and David both exhaled and gave each other a nod. Their ability to keep cool while having someone approach that was armed was vital to their survival.

They waited until the guys were out of sight before telling the girls to come back up on the deck.

"I hate these close calls. I hate feeling like I can't trust anyone. It just seems like such a waste that we can't figure out how to help each other instead of always feeling like someone is trying to take advantage of us," John said.

"I agree, but it's just too hard to tell these days. We don't know where people's intentions are anymore and you have to assume that people are actually bad instead of good. It sucks, but there's nothing we can do about it. We have to be on the offensive if we are going to survive," David said.

"Do you think he was right about a FEMA camp at Herman? Do you think that maybe they will allow us

STRIKE POINT: ADRIFT

some fuel and food? I don't want to become a prisoner again," John asked.

"I have a feeling we'll be just fine. Let's just say, I have a golden ticket," David replied.

CHAPTER 9

It wasn't long before we came upon the bridge and landing at Hermann. Hitting the boat landing was difficult, but David managed to get us there. The soldiers saw his uniform and acknowledged his rank.

"Welcome, Sergeant," the uniformed men said as they saluted and then pulled our boat to shore, tying it off.

We weren't sure if we were going to be welcomed and assisted or if we would have to somehow defend ourselves, so we picked up our packs and weapons to take with us.

"Welcome to Hermann. You can find food and water if you don't mind walking a little way," said one of the soldiers.

"Thank you, just point the way," David replied.

He got the directions of where the camp was and we began to head south on the main road that met up with the bridge.

STRIKE POINT: ADRIFT

"I didn't know you were a Sergeant," I said.

"It doesn't matter. You're a civilian," David replied.

While that actually made sense, I would have thought he would have mentioned it before.

"So, are we going to take our chances at another FEMA camp?" I asked, unsure if this was a wise decision after the previous situation.

"I don't think we'll have a problem here. It's not like it was in Tipton. I briefly chatted with the guard and they do not have the same rules here. Plus, I have something that will help us if we get into a jam," David replied.

"Yeah, you said something about a golden ticket?" I asked.

David smiled and nodded, but did not reveal what this golden ticket supposedly was. I just decided to trust him since he seemed to know what he was doing.

"Do you think they'll give us fuel? Obviously, they said food and water are here, but will we be able to get any gasoline?" I asked.

"I'm sure we will. I'm not sure how much they can give us, but hopefully it will be enough to get us to St. Louis without any kind of issue," David replied.

As we made our way along the road, we couldn't help but notice the historical buildings that looked like they hadn't been touched in a century. It was apparent that the townspeople had chosen to try to keep the charm intact.

We walked about half a mile up the road, passing many quaint historical looking buildings until we were at a location that had been set up with several tents and what looked like food trucks. My stomach responded to the scent of freshly cooked meat.

"Do I smell barbecue?" Laura said, her eyes wide as mine.

EMERSON HAWK

"Yeah, the guard said that there was plenty of food here, and that we would have access to it," David said.

"But how will they pay for all of this? I mean, they had to get it from somewhere and somebody had to get paid, right?" Lisa asked.

That was a good question. I wondered how they were able to have a barbecue truck or any other kind of food truck for that matter. And how were people paying for the food?

The camp was open aired and there were no fences anywhere. It was surprisingly different than what we had witnessed in Tipton. This wasn't like a prison, this was open for people to come and go as they needed. It was a delightful change from what we had experienced before.

People were working together to create a feeling of warmth and welcome. As we made our way in through the main area, an elderly lady came over to us and asked us if we needed any help.

"I smell something that smells like barbecue. Where is it and how can I get some?" Laura asked the old lady.

The old lady pointed towards a couple of rows of food trucks that were all set up to take orders, just like if we were in some type of amusement park. We made our way over and decided to see what was available to eat.

We were all still astonished at how this was able to be pulled off since money wasn't working anymore.

As I stopped and gazed at the menu, it became obvious how things were working. Instead of cash, people were accepting other things that could be used for payment. Gold, silver and ammunition were at the top of the list. You could barter if you had some other kind of food to trade. Alcohol and cigarettes were always welcome, as was weed or any kind of prescription or other

STRIKE POINT: ADRIFT

drugs.

"Well, I wished I smoked or had something to drink. As it stands, the only thing I have is ammunition and I really don't want to give up any of it right now," I said to Laura.

"Uh-huh. And how hungry will you need to be before you start to eat your bullets?" Laura asked me.

"I'm not sure yet, babe. I'm hungry now, but we still have a long way to go. I just don't know about this," I replied. We needed to keep as much ammo as we could. We just didn't know what might lay ahead.

David came up to us and huddled us together. "Listen, you guys can use some of your ammunition to buy food. I will be able to get us more. So don't worry about it. Trust me on this," David said, and smiled as he backed away, pulling out a few bullets to use for a giant hamburger that he wanted.

Laura and I looked at each other as we quickly dropped our bags and searched for what we had. Laura took out ten rounds of 9 mm from her box and went over to the barbecued rib truck. I decided that a smoked half chicken would be my saving grace. We both met back up over at one of the picnic tables under a tree.

Lisa and David joined us with their choices and we all sat around and filled our bellies. It was almost like we were at some kind of picnic. So far, we had been fortunate that we had yet to really experience any true hunger, and for that I was grateful.

"Is there any place around that we can pick up some high-protein bars or granola bars to carry along? Or nuts and seeds? Something that is lightweight and that we can eat on the way without needing water for having to cook it?" I asked David.

"I'm sure they'll be plenty of choices. Let's finish

here and make our way over to the main tent where I can get us set up with fuel and rations to take with us," David said.

We watched as other people came and went with different offerings for food. I wondered about those people who had nothing to offer in exchange. What happened to them? Were they just allowed to starve?

"Baby, what happens if someone can't pay for some of this food?" Lisa asked David before I could get the words out.

David looked at all of us before answering. "They have to work it off. If they want food, you have to either work for it or pay for it. There is no free ride. Not anymore. So you will have to give either some labor or some type of payment in today's new currency. And we can already see what that currency is," David replied.

Sometimes, I found David's matter-of-fact nature a little off-putting, but I figured it was because of the time he'd spent in the military.

We finished our food and relaxed as David went to speak to the commanding officers. We decided to do a little bit of exploration.

As we made our way through the downtown area, we came to a clearing where several people were working in a park that had been turned into a garden. You could tell that a lot of it was pretty new and recently installed. It was quite busy with people hoeing and weeding.

Some of the people were senior citizens that looked like they could barely walk, much less work a field. Laura and I were confused at how they could allow these senior citizens to do this kind of labor in the heat.

We noticed several guards that were carrying weapons and surrounding the perimeter, almost as if they

STRIKE POINT: ADRIFT

were watching the people working to make sure that they didn't stop. I knew this was speculation on my part, but it just appeared to be cruel to these seniors.

"Is this what David was talking about? That, in order to be fed, these poor old people have to be out here hoeing and picking weeds so that they can eat?" Laura asked.

"I don't know. This could be something completely different. Let's not assume anything at this point. It could be that the seniors chose to come out here, and they asked the guards to watch out for anyone trying to raid their garden," I replied.

"I couldn't imagine my grandma out in this heat, working like a dog," Lisa injected. Laura reached over and patted her on the shoulder as we walked back towards the main area and back over to the picnic table under the tree.

David returned shortly thereafter and told us that we would have a full tank of fuel by morning. But we would have to stay the night and we would have to do something in return for the fuel.

"And what might that be?" Laura said, putting her hands on her hips and giving him a side-eyed look.

"You'll have to be witnesses to my wedding," David replied as Lisa's eyes got wide and she flung her arms around his neck.

CHAPTER 10

The white gravel path almost seemed to glow as the firelight from the torches on either side lit the way from the bed and breakfast to the gazebo. David stood on the platform next to the preacher, trying not to show his anxieties.

The moon was rising full and bright, and the warm spring breeze promised to help wick away the sweat coming off of David's neck.

Laura took the ring off that Ben had given her and placed it in David's hand. "Here, take this."

"I can't take this. This was a gift from Ben," David said, looking at the gold band in his hand.

"Then just use it until you can pick something out for her later." Laura smiled as she made her way back down to her chair.

David looked at the ring and slipped it into his pocket as he smiled and winked at Laura.

"Thank you. Thank you for being my friend and being here for Lisa. She really cares a lot about you...like a sister," David said. Laura's heart was warmed by the thought.

Their conversation was interrupted by John and Lisa coming out of the bed and breakfast and down the stairs towards them. One of the ladies had given Lisa a dress to wear. It was many sizes too big, but was pinned in the back to make it fit. She linked her arm through John's as they walked up the gravel path.

John took Lisa's hand and placed it into David's as he stepped down and took a seat next to Laura. John and Laura watched quietly as the preacher began his normal marriage vow speech.

"Who'da thought we'd be attending a wedding in the middle of the apocalypse?" Laura whispered into John's ear as they both watched the lovebirds swoon.

"I now pronounce you husband and wife. You may kiss the bride," the preacher announced with a smile as he closed his Bible and gave them a nod. Laura couldn't help but shed a few tears.

Lisa and David kissed and he picked her up, twirling her around. Her joyful laugh filled the air, and things almost felt normal.

Laura and John stood up and went over to congratulate them, giving them hugs and well wishes as if the world had never changed. The preacher left and the four of them decided that no matter what, they would always be friends forever.

"I'm so glad that you were all here. This has been very special to me. You are my family," Lisa said with a tear in her eyes as she looked down at the ring on her hand. "This was the ring that Ben gave you, wasn't it?"

Laura nodded. "You keep it until you guys can pick up something special for yourselves."

EMERSON HAWK

Lisa hugged Laura and smiled. One of the ladies of the bed and breakfast came out onto the porch and called to them to come over.

"Mrs. Elliot, if you would do me the honor?" David said with his best British accent, holding his arm out for Lisa to link in.

They walk down the torch lit path and up onto the porch of the huge house. There was a small table with a white linen tablecloth that had a small bouquet of roses, a plate of fresh strawberries, and four champagne flutes bubbling with white champagne.

"What's this?" David asked the hostess.

"There won't be too many times that we'll be able to do this before we run out of champagne or fresh strawberries. We wanted to make it special for you. Enjoy it, and we wish you the best in your marriage and in life. It's just our way of saying that we hope you have a happy life together," the hostess said, smiling before disappearing back inside.

They all picked up a glass and clinked them together. "Here's to long lives and happiness," John said.

They all took a drink of the bubbly liquid before grabbing a fresh gigantic strawberry and enjoying its clean sweetness.

"She said that we all can have a room in the house, as long as we make sure to leave it clean when we leave. We can stay here for the night, instead of staying at the camp," Laura said.

"Really? That's awesome!" Lisa replied, giddy as if she had just won some kind of prize.

They all realized just how special this was, because the only other option was to take a cot back at the camp.

They spent the evening out on the front porch enjoying each other's company and trying not to think

STRIKE POINT: ADRIFT

about what lay ahead. It was always easy for them to get caught up in the thoughts of all of the bad things that could be waiting for them. But not tonight. Tonight was a celebration of love and of friendship.

CHAPTER 11

The sun pushed its way into the window through the sheer curtains and forced me to open my eyes. I was so comfortable that I just didn't want to get up at all. I knew we had a long day ahead of us and we really wanted to try to get back on the river and back towards home as soon as possible.

Last night was spent enjoying each other's company and celebrating the marriage of David and Lisa. It was nice to not think much about the bad side of this messy world. I rolled over and gently stroked Laura's hair, causing her to wake up.

"Man, this bed is more comfortable than the one at Ben's house. And I thought that was the best bed I'd ever slept in," Laura yawned and stretched awake.

"I know what you mean. I wish in some ways we could just stay here."

Before the wedding, we'd all had the opportunity to shower so we were all clean and the hostess had even

STRIKE POINT: ADRIFT

washed our clothes from us being in the river the day before.

"I wonder how they are doing the laundry? I'm curious to see if they are using some kind of machine or doing it manually," Laura said. Her interests were now in new ways to do chores without electricity.

We packed our bags and made our way downstairs, the smell of coffee and fresh breakfast catching our attention. "Good morning. I hope you're hungry. We just finished making breakfast. Please, come and eat," our hostess said.

We went down into the dining room where David and Lisa were already sitting. They were bright eyed and bushy tailed, which was surprising considering they probably were up most of the night.

"How did you sleep?" Laura's sheepish grin told us she wasn't really interested in how they slept.

Lisa sighed heavily and looked up at the ceiling with a dreamy expression. She really didn't need to answer that question. David just blushed as he buttered his toast and shoved it in his mouth to keep from having to answer.

"Well, we slept really good. And this breakfast looks amazing," I said as I looked at the spread of food on the table.

"How is it we are able to eat this good here? I mean, it's not like we are royalty," Laura asked.

"Well, it has to do with this golden ticket I have," David grinned.

"Okay, what is it with this golden ticket? You keep talking about it but you have yet to reveal what it actually is. So what gives?" I finally pushed to find out what this was about.

He reached in his front pocket and pulled out a

piece of paper, handing it to me. I opened it up and began to read.

It was a letter from General Knox, stating that David was on a special mission for the military and that his job was to get all of us back to St. Louis because we were very important people.

I began to chuckle and looked up at David. "And how did you manage this? Important people?"

David nodded, taking another bite of fresh cantaloupe. "Uh-huh, and it wasn't even my idea. It was Knox's idea to give me that, in case we ran into anyone else that might give us some trouble. He wanted to make sure that as we traveled, we would be treated with respect because of our commitment to doing the right thing back in Tipton."

I folded up the letter and gave it back to him. He shoved it back into his front pocket.

"Works for me. I kinda like this treatment." I grabbed a fresh strawberry and popped it into my mouth, savoring its tang.

"So do I. I could live like this all the time. It almost doesn't feel like the apocalypse," Laura jested.

We finished our breakfast and gathered our things, making sure to thank our hostess for treating us so wonderfully.

After stopping at the tent where the commander was in charge, we loaded up our weapons and ammo and were given several days of rations and water. We were all set to go. They even filled up the boat with fuel. That must have been quite a feat, considering the tank was at least twenty gallons.

I stood at the boat ramp and looked back over the town, relishing in its old-fashioned quaintness. A lot of the original buildings had been restored to their origi-

STRIKE POINT: ADRIFT

nal glory and it felt as if it had been taken back in time, before there actually was electricity.

In my mind, I thought that this would be a great place to live if the city didn't work out for us. Of course, we still had the option to go back to Ben's house, should we ever choose to. We boarded the boat and shoved off, waving goodbye to our hosts.

"So, now that we have a full tank, how long do you think it will take us to get to St. Louis?" I asked.

"Actually, now that we're filled up if we go full blast, it should take us less than a couple of hours, barring any unforeseen problems," David replied with a smile. David and Lisa were still in their own euphoria from the night before. It was nice to see them happy.

David opened the throttle wide and we flew down river. It was exhilarating as the wind and the spray from the river spread cool moisture across my face. It felt like we were just having a day out on the water and had just finished camping.

The girls sat down in the boat and David and I took turns steering as we watched the shore line on both sides pass us by.

However, our enjoyment was short lived. As we made our way closer to the bridge at Washington, we noticed several boats that were lined up right underneath its shadow. David throttled down the engine, so we could see what was ahead.

"What do you think this is about?" I asked.

"Girls, go below quickly," David said, his voice taking command. "I'm not sure what this is about, but it doesn't look good. There are quite a few of them and some of their boats are faster than ours."

As we drew closer, we could see that several ropes had been strung between the footings of the bridge.

EMERSON HAWK

If a boat had tried to go through, it would have easily flipped the boat up into the air and taken out anyone that was inside. The only things that might have made it through would have been a large barge. David pushed the throttle down and let it idle as we got closer.

I recognized two of the men from before. It was the two middle eastern men that had circled us and told us about Hermann.

"Oh, this isn't good," I said under my breath.

David readied his pistol and I brought up my rifle. We both looked over the line of boats and noticed that almost all the men appeared to be Arabic, with a few white and black men interspersed. They looked like they had been plucked from one of those gang shows I used to see on TV.

"Where might you be going?" It was the same man who circled us before.

"We told you already, St. Louis. That's where were heading," David replied.

My gut told me that this was going to get ugly. We needed to turn back before something bad happened. There was just too many of them for us to defend against.

"Let's get out of here. This isn't worth it. I don't want to risk our lives here. Let's go back to Hermann and we can find another way or get some assistance," I said.

David nodded and turned the boat around to go back up river. He began to push the throttle up, but quickly realized we had been surrounded by several more boats with heavily armed men.

We could try to outrun them, but they all had their weapons drawn and readied. We weren't going anywhere.

CHAPTER 12

Two of the boats came alongside and we were boarded quickly. There was a lot of conversation in a language I did not understand, but it sounded like it was Arabic. Our guns were seized and the girls were found. We were taken to the landing under the bridge and forced off the boat.

Our supplies were taken and we were led up a paved path to some type of encampment. I tried to make a mental note of the faces and any names that I could, so that I could write them down for someone later, but it was impossible. I couldn't understand them.

The girls were surprisingly quiet, although David and I could both tell how scared they were.

We walked about half a mile parallel to the river through a path in the forest that led to a clearing where a bunch of tents had been set up. In the middle of the tents, was a large farmhouse that was well guarded. There was a circle drive that encompassed a large grassy

EMERSON HAWK

area where someone had created a large fire pit that was smoldering from the night before.

"On your knees!" one of the men said as the other men in the camp began to gather around us. It took us a moment before we realized just how serious this was about to become. The intensity in which my anxiety was rising was making me feel almost dizzy.

We were forced into a lineup. David and I were on the outside and Laura and Lisa in between us. One of the men cocked his gun and put it to Laura's head. She yelped in surprise and began shaking uncontrollably.

"You won't make me ask twice," he said in broken English as Laura quickly dropped to her knees and we all followed.

The door of the farmhouse opened and out came a very tall man who was wearing some kind of uniform I didn't recognize. His demeanor was one of power and prestige. Whoever he was, he was the highest ranking among these individuals.

We stayed on our knees for several moments before I noticed that on the flagpole wasn't the American flag that I would have expected to see. Instead, it was the black flag of ISIS. My heart sank as I looked around and realized that we had been infiltrated. I wasn't sure how it happened, but this was a Jihadi camp.

"So, I've been told you are trying to get to St. Louis?" the man asked as he paced back and forth in front of us. None of us responded. We just stared at him as we all tried to make sense of what was happening.

"Oh, I'm sorry. I guess I should introduce myself. My name is Sayid Ashraf," he said.

He walked past me with an air of arrogance as he turned sharply and went back the other direction, looking down his nose. Then, he went back to the center and

STRIKE POINT: ADRIFT

faced all of us.

"It would be wise for you to listen to me very carefully. We have taken over this country. It no longer belongs to you. It belongs to Allah. We are his servants and we have to come to transform it into a nation that serves him and Islam."

I couldn't believe what I was hearing. Not on American soil. I carefully glanced over at David who was turning fifty shades of red as he listened to this man spout off.

"We have been quietly taking over your cities little by little with the help of your government. Your government has been very good to Islam. They have welcomed us with open arms and we have been able to easily cross the borders without question. Your government has given us money and food. They have given us land and even helped us open businesses, and given us positions of power. We are grateful to your government for helping us to position ourselves to come in and replace your laws with Sharia Law," Sayid boasted, as he raised his hands and face to the sky.

Laura's face was covered in tears as she listened to Sayid ramble on. I carefully eyed the men who were watching the spectacle. There had to be at least forty, if not more.

"In order to keep your lives, you will have to profess your faith to Allah," Sayid continued.

My mind was in a tailspin as his words began to fall into the background. All I could think of, was all of the news stories I had heard about where ISIS had beheaded people for not being Muslim. How they had crucified Christians and burned alive people who would not believe in this so called 'religion of peace'.

"Take them away!" I heard him say, as I was pulled

EMERSON HAWK

out of my thoughts by two men pulling me up off the ground and away from Laura.

"John! John!" Laura yelled as they took her and Lisa to the back side of the house.

David and I were taken over to two bamboo cages and forced inside. After locking the cages, they were both hoisted up into the trees, high enough that if we could even make it out, we'd probably break an ankle trying to jump.

How could this have happened? Was it true that ISIS had been able to take over the whole country? Maybe David was wrong and it wasn't our own government who'd had a hand in the EMPs. Maybe our government had been taken over and they'd had no choice but to comply?

I would never know the truth, and neither would most people in this country. We only knew what we could see. And right now, we could see that surviving the EMPs was probably the least of our worries.

CHAPTER 13

ow I knew how birds felt. The heat of the day began to wear on us as we sat in our swinging cages.

"You don't happen to have a golden ticket that will work with Sayid, do you?" I asked, in a dehydrated haze.

After many hours, we had become quite thirsty. The Muslims in the camp would come by and taunt us with water and yell "Allahu Akbar," trying to get a rise out of us. They'd throw water on us and watching as we'd lick off whatever landed on our skin.

"I need to get out of this cage. If I can get out, I might be able to save the girls," David whispered when there was no one around.

"How will you do that? We have no weapons," I asked.

"I have special training," David replied.

"Oh yeah? What kind of special training?"

"The kind where you learn to kill people with your

bare hands," he replied.

"I wish you'd have taught me," I said.

"Yeah, I should have. I just never thought I would actually need to use it in here in this country."

The day turned into night and we struggled to get comfortable in our hanging prisons. Even if we could sleep, our minds were only on one thing. Escape.

David was full of rage and anger as he watched the camp closely, trying to figure out who was in charge of whom and who he wanted to take down after Sayid.

"I need to get to Sayid first. If I can take him down, at least we might be able to disrupt the group enough to get out and save the girls."

I really began to worry about the girls. My mind went to places it didn't want to go with what little I knew of the Muslims and how they treated women in general.

Muslim men viewed women as property. I remembered seeing some news articles about Europe and Greece having to deal with the influx of rapes from the refugees they'd graciously taken into their countries.

Mainstream media never reported on how the countries would open their arms to the refugees, only to have their women raped and the refugees defying all of their laws. It was too late when they'd realized it'd been a huge mistake.

I remembered Laura wondering how the governments of those countries could allow it to happen. She said how glad she was that at least here in America, something like that most likely would be met with force from the citizens.

I wasn't sure if this here was something going on all across the nation, but I feared it was. Small pockets of Muslims quietly going about their lives, unaware that they would be forced to kill their non-Muslim neigh-

STRIKE POINT: ADRIFT

bors when the time came.

This country has failed its citizens. In our country's desire to be politically correct, it had allowed hundreds of thousands of Jihadis, disguised as refugees, to flood past our borders totally unchecked.

Now, America was being taken over.

I couldn't hold back my tears and anger at how our government had let us down. I wondered how much David knew of this atrocity.

"Did you know?" I asked.

"Know what?" David replied.

"Did you know that the Jihadis were coming in to take over?"

David shook his head. "No. And most of my comrades didn't know. This is way higher than most of us knew about. Assuming that it's even true."

"What do you mean?" I asked.

"Just because Sayid says it happened, doesn't mean it's true. You can't let him win the mental game he's playing. He's working on our minds. That's what all leaders do. They get you to believe that there is no way but their way," David replied.

"But what if he is telling the truth? What if America is now going to be forced to become a Muslim country?"

"Even if that is what they are trying to do, it'll never happen. Sure, maybe there will be pockets like this one. But they'll never take over completely. Our guys won't have it. We've been fighting these sand people for way too long. Trust me, John. Don't let his words get into your soul and rob you of your patriotism."

David was right. I was letting Sayid's words work their way into my brain and twist it all around. I needed to stay strong.

The night was long as we watched the Arabs get

drunk and belligerent. Sayid came out and sat on the front porch of the farmhouse where he oversaw his men with a glass of wine. They had built a large fire in the middle of the grassy area that glowed all around the camp.

"I thought Muslims didn't drink," I said to David.

"That's what most people think. They usually just stick to wine. But they do drink. It's okay in some groups and not in others. Just like with Christianity, some people think it's okay to drink and others don't," David replied.

I watched and waited to see if they all were going to get drunk enough to pass out. I hoped that Sayid would also be drinking so that perhaps David and I could find a way to break free and we could rescue the girls and get out of there.

But my hopes were soon dashed as I saw several women being pulled out into the main gathering area. As I looked at the women in the firelight I didn't see Lisa or Laura. I didn't know where they were. But there were several women being abused right in front of us. It was as if it was okay to use these women, who were non-Muslim, in any way the men saw fit.

Several of the women tried to resist and were beaten and slapped down with fists while we watched in horror. Their cries and screams made my blood boil.

"I want to kill them. I want to kill them all," I said out loud to no one in particular. All I could think of was that this was not the way we should be treating other humans. This was not the way.

"Don't worry, you'll get your chance. Trust me," David growled.

CHAPTER 14

Laura and Lisa had been taken into one of the tents at the back of the compound. There were several women inside that were dressed in the hijab and the typical Muslim women's clothing, where the only thing that you could see was a slit for their eyes. Laura and Lisa both noticed several cages surrounding the back part of the tent where women were being held.

The caged women were wearing very little clothing and you could tell they had been beaten. Laura and Lisa were shoved into one of the cages next to the other captured women.

They were both frightened and scared at what might happen. Laura knew that John would do whatever it took to keep her from being harmed, but she also realized that in the current circumstances, John may not be able to save them.

"How long have you been here?" Laura asked one young woman who was sitting in the cage next to her.

EMERSON HAWK

Timid and scared, the girl was afraid to speak. She waited until the Muslim women went to the front of the tent, then peeked around Laura and Lisa to make sure she couldn't be seen.

"I don't know. I can't remember. We've been here so long and don't know what day it is. All I know is that I've been here since the blackout," the young girl said.

"How old are you?" Lisa asked her.

"Nineteen," she replied.

"We have to get out of here. We have to find a way to get out," Lisa said quietly.

"If you try to escape, they will kill you. If you want to live, you'll do what they say and not ask questions. You'll do everything they tell you to. You're going to want to fight. Don't do it. They'll slit your throat." The fear in the young girl's eyes was palpable.

Laura wanted to ask more questions, but the Muslim women came over and began yelling at them and banging the cage with bamboo sticks, poking through and pushing them around the cage.

"You will do as I say. You will follow my rules. If you do not, I will make you wish you were dead. Do not defy me," the Muslim woman said to Laura and Lisa.

Her English was surprisingly good. She didn't have the Arabic accent that they had heard from the men. This woman was obviously well educated or perhaps American.

Laura decided to try to find out what was going to happen to them. She walked up to the front of the cage and looked into the lady's eyes.

"What are you going to do with us? Why are you keeping us prisoner? We have done nothing to you," Laura asked.

The lady took her stick and pushed Laura back further into the cage, rapping it on her fingers and poking her to force her back.

"You do not question. You just listen and obey, or you die," the lady said.

Lisa and Laura sat down and huddled together, crying as they realized their fate. Laura realized that these women were just there to be used for the men's sexual desires. They would be raped at will and only be fed just enough to keep them alive.

Laura remembered reading about the rapes that were happening on the other side of the world. How the countries that allowed the refugees to flood their borders were being taken over by young men who'd chosen not to integrate with their host countries.

There were reports of many women being raped who had previously welcomed the refugees. It was a harsh wake-up call for them to realize that their country was being taken over by men who thought nothing more of women than something they could screw and kill if they wanted. It was savagery at its worst.

Another lady who was dressed in Muslim garb came into the tent and spoke something in Arabic to the lead woman. She came over and opened the cage, pulling Laura out and locking it back behind her.

Laura tried to run, but the other women stopped her and hit her several times with heavy bamboo canes until she fell to the ground and covered her head, screaming. The pain of the heavy cane immediately bruised Laura's back and legs.

"You do not run. You will obey," the woman in black said.

They forced Laura outside and around to the front of the house. She frantically looked around to see if she could find John or David, and only noticed them up

EMERSON HAWK

in the hanging cages as she was being pulled into the house.

"John!" she yelled out, getting his attention and his eyes met hers just as she disappeared into the house.

She didn't know how she was going to get out of this, but she didn't like where this was going. The women took her upstairs and into the bathroom where they stripped her naked and forced her to bathe. Anytime she would try to resist, they would slap and beat her.

They washed and braided her hair and put some kind of strange smelling oils on her body.

"How can you live like this? How can you allow these men to use you this way? There is a better way. You do not have to be slaves," Laura cried as she begged the women to stop.

Laura was spun around by the force of the back of a hand, slapping her across the face. The metallic taste of the blood in her mouth made her more than aware that she may very well die tonight. As she brought her head up, she saw herself in the mirror, naked and afraid.

She began to sob as she realized that she wouldn't be able to stop the process. She prayed that if this were to be her fate, that she wouldn't hate God for allowing this to happen to her.

They took Laura and put her in a sheer gown that did nothing to hide her body. There was a large bedroom at the end of the hallway that had been lit with candles. There was nothing else inside, except a large bed.

"You will wait here for Sayid. He will come to see you when it is time for him. You will wait here until he arrives," the lady in black said, and she closed the door behind Laura.

Laura immediately began looking for a way out. She went over to the window, but it was on the second floor

STRIKE POINT: ADRIFT

and she could see guards standing around below. Even if she could make the jump without breaking a bone, the guards would surely kill her.

There was a closet that was locked, but nothing else for her to use to defend herself. As she sat down on the foot of the bed, she thought about her situation and how many millions of women were raped by these animals.

She remembered reading part of the Quran and how it spoke of women being nothing more than property that the men owned. That they could be used as the men saw fit. It was sickening to her and she knew that she was not the only one who would have to go through this kind of torture.

She worried that he would beat her or cut her, and tried not to think about that. She decided that if she was going to survive, the best thing for her to do was to comply and not fight back. Perhaps by complying, she would live another day to try to find a way out.

Against everything in her body, she knew she would have to let this creep have his way with her, if she was going to survive.

What seemed like hours was only minutes when Laura heard the sound of footsteps and the door being unlocked and opened. She stood to her feet as Sayid entered the room and locked the door behind him.

Sayid didn't say anything as he just stood there for a moment, and looked at her.

She didn't move. She stood silently, but stared directly into his eyes. She wanted to let him know that she was not his subservient slave like the other women. She maintained eye contact with him as long as possible.

He walked over to one corner of the room and began to unbutton his shirt. As he peeled off his clothing, she could see that he was muscle bound and looked very strong. She feared that if she resisted him, that he would easily be able to strangle her or break her neck.

Her trembling was taking over as she could not stop the fear from coursing through her. She stood tall and proud as she watched him in silence.

He walked over to her and grabbed her by the throat, gently squeezing against the arteries in her neck, causing her face to flush red from the pressure and she swallowed hard as she stared him down, trying not to pass out.

"You American women think you are strong and should to be in control. That is not how it will be in the future. You will be owned by Islam. Allah has spoken of this, and it is the way it will be," Sayid stated as he released her throat.

Laura chose not to speak, even though the words were burning on her tongue, trying to escape her mouth. She knew that no matter what she said, there was no convincing this monster that he was evil. It would be like trying to tell the devil that he was doing the wrong thing. There just was no reasoning with this kind of person.

Laura stood firm and continued to stare him down. Not allowing him to intimidate her with his words. She didn't know if that was the right thing to do, but it was all that she had left to fight with.

Sayid came back over to her and ripped off the gown that she had been wearing, forcing her to instinctively try to cover herself with her hands.

Sayid laughed out loud, "The whore tries to hide herself. That is so funny. You American women are so funny."

Laura's blood boiled. She knew better than to open her mouth, but it was almost too much. His insults and

STRIKE POINT: ADRIFT

comments were pushing her limits.

She didn't want to be beaten. She knew what was coming already. She had no control over that, but she could keep her tongue and might be able to live long enough to rescue Lisa, John or David.

"Get up on the bed. On all fours, like the bitch you are. I feel like fucking a dog tonight," Sayid commanded.

Laura's heart dropped into her stomach and her eyes filled with tears as she slowly turned around and got onto the bed on all fours, her backside facing the monster that was about to violate her.

Sayid came over to the bed and grabbed the side of her hip, pulling her towards his crotch. "Good... Good doggie. At least this bitch knows how to obey."

Laura couldn't take any more of his pontificating. She'd had enough and didn't care anymore about living or dying. She just wanted to be free. As he began to get on the bed behind her, she turned quickly and did a donkey kick, crushing his manhood as hard as she could with her foot, screaming as she did.

Sayid fell backwards onto the floor, grabbing his manhood and yelling at her in some Arabic gibberish that she couldn't understand.

She jumped up off the bed and grabbed one of the candles that had been burning and was full of hot wax. Slinging it towards him, the hot wax landed on the side of his face, burning him.

When he got to his feet, Laura couldn't move away fast enough and his hand came down hard on her face. He slapped her so hard that she spun around and collapsed to the floor like a rag doll, as it knocked her out cold.

He bent down to grab Laura by the hair, but was interrupted by a hard knock on the door. There was some

EMERSON HAWK

commotion that forced him to stop what he was doing, and he left her lifeless body lying on the floor.

"I'll be back to deal with you later!" Sayid yelled, slamming the door behind him.

CHAPTER 15

Adrenaline does weird thing to the body. It could give you energy or cause your muscles to seize. At the moment, it was doing both to me.

After seeing Sayid follow Laura inside the house, I knew he was either going to rape her or kill her, and there was nothing I could do to stop it. I reached up and began to push against all the bars of the cage, trying to find a way to wiggle something free. It was tightly made. Unless I had access to some kind of knife, I wasn't going anywhere.

"I have to get out of here. I have to find a way to get her," I said to David.

"I know, brother. I'm working on it."

I continued to watch the men below as they openly violated the other women that apparently had been kept locked up wherever Lisa and Laura had been. I suspected that after Sayid got done using any of the newly captured, he gave them to his men to use however they saw fit.

The animalistic nature of these people was something that I was not mentally prepared to deal with. I sat helplessly in my cage and cried, as I thought about my Laura being so horribly violated.

David and I were roused by a commotion of people that had come into the camp. The bonfire and the additional torches lit things up enough to be able to see that there were three people that had been tied up and were forced into the center of the grassy area.

It appeared to be a family. A man, woman and a young girl.

The front door of the house opened and Sayid strolled out, straightening his pants and pulling his shirt back on. My stomach went cold and turned into a rock as I envisioned what he had been doing to Laura. All I wanted to do at that moment was strangled him with my bare hands, until the life left his eyes.

"Well now, it looks like our hosts have returned. So glad of you to join us," Sayid said sarcastically as the man, woman and child were forced onto their knees in the middle of the grass in front of the house.

David and I were watching intently as he looked at the man's face. Sayid looked over at us and made some command to his soldiers. They came over and brought down our cages from the trees. Pulling us out of our cages, they brought us to face the poor family and pushed us down to our knees. David and I had no idea what was about to happen.

"These people used to live here. They graciously accepted us into their home when we emigrated. They treated us like family, except they are not Muslim. We tried to convince them to convert to Islam, but they refused. They chose to stick with their fake Christian

STRIKE POINT: ADRIFT

beliefs. Once the power went out and we took control, we gave them the choice to convert," Sayid said as he walked around the three people.

I looked at the mother and the young girl who had to have been about ten years old. They were crying and trembling, and were barely keeping their bodies upright. My heart ached for them as much as for Laura.

"We tried to get them to understand that this country will be owned by Islam and Sharia Law will rule America. But they disagreed and chose to run away. We knew that we could not allow them to live any longer, as Mohammad and Sharia Law commands us to kill the infidels. Anyone who does not convert is an infidel, according to the Quran," Sayid continued.

Sayid pulled out a large knife that flashed when the light of the fire hit it.

"Allah thanks you for giving us your property and being kind to us, but he does not forgive those who will not convert," Sayid said before grabbing the man's head and pulling the knife across his throat, severing his head from his body in three or four strokes.

Fear is strange and does things to the body you cannot control. I felt as though I was in some sort of horror movie and someone had drugged me. I could barely maintain my upright position as I saw Sayid lift the head up in the air and the men in the camp yelled, "Allahu Akbar" in unison.

His wife and daughter began screaming at the top of their lungs and David and I tried to stand. We were forced back down to our knees by several men as we were forced to watch. I cried as I lowered my head and prayed for this to end.

The mother couldn't handle what she saw and fell face forward into the grass, passing out from fear. The

EMERSON HAWK

young girl just kept screaming.

"Lift the woman up!" Sayid said to his men as they pulled her off the ground, her head hanging down as she was still passed out. The young girl screamed over and over and begged and pleaded with them not to kill her mother.

"Please, I promise to do anything that you say. Please do not kill my mother," the young girl cried.

"Oh, how true you speak. You will do whatever we say. Because if you do not, you will suffer the same fate," Sayid said as he lifted the mother's head and took it off with a few strokes from his knife, the blood spurting out and landing on the young girl's leg.

The woman's body was released and fell to the ground as her head was tossed next to it. I could not believe what I was seeing. I felt like I was in some kind of nightmare.

I tried to hold back my sobs and looked over at David who was so angry that he was shaking, tears rolling down his face, his jaw locked tight.

David and I knew that we were in a volatile situation. We had to find a way to survive this at all costs, if we were going to be able to come back and kill this bastard.

We watched the men laugh as they pulled the young girl to her feet and dragged her back to the tent behind the house, where we figured Lisa and Laura were being kept.

David and I could barely keep our bodies upright as we watched the animals take the bodies and heads, dragging them out into the woods to leave for the wild animals.

"You Americans are so stupid. Our Quran teaches us to lie if we have to, in order to further Islam. It is

STRIKE POINT: ADRIFT

called Taqiyya. Sharia Law commands that if we have to pretend to be your friend, and even pretend to be moderate to continue the furtherance of Islam, then we are to use whatever means necessary, including lying to those who are not Muslim," Sayid boasted.

"Your people have welcomed us with open arms and allowed us to infiltrate into every nook and cranny of your country. Now that Allah has called us into action, no Muslim will be allowed to ignore their calling. Even those who have been peaceful for so long, must follow the Quran."

I tried to listen to him rant, but all I could really think about was getting free and saving Laura.

Sayid continued his speech. "And the Quran says that anyone who does not follow Allah must be killed or be a slave. There is no such thing as a moderate Muslim. All Muslims are either true followers of Islam or are infidels and will either be slaves or killed," Sayid stated.

Whether we wanted it or not, we were getting an education on what these savages believed. How could we have been so blind?

"Now that you have seen what happens to infidels, you have a choice. You can either pledge your lives to Allah and follow Islam or you can meet the same fate of this family," Sayid said.

Sayid gave some kind of command to his men and we were dragged back to our cages and pulled back up over the camp. I could barely move from the exhaustion and dehydration.

There was no way that I planned on converting to Islam. But if I had to, I would lie to keep us alive, until I had the opportunity to gut this animal from groin to gullet.

CHAPTER 16

The young girl who had just watched her parents' beheading was dragged back into the tent with the other women and pushed into the cage with Lisa.

The women pushed her in and gave her water that she sipped, but immediately vomited back up.

Lisa instinctively reached out to her and pulled her close, holding her as she trembled violently and sobbed hard into Lisa's chest.

"What have you people done? Why is this child scared to death?" Lisa yelled at the Muslim women, noticing the blood all over the girl's legs.

"It is not for you to question the ways of Islam. You only need to obey and be quiet," said one of the other Muslim women.

The Muslim women handed out small pieces of bread to each of the caged women and small cup of water that everyone eagerly drank and ate.

STRIKE POINT: ADRIFT

"You must eat. It may be all you get for a while. You will need to keep your strength as much as possible to survive," one of the caged women whispered to Lisa.

Lisa looked over at the other women and was amazed at how emaciated they all were. They obviously had been starved the entire time they had been here.

"Where's your brother?" said one girl to the young girl that was in the cage with Lisa. "Did he escape?"

The young girl that was with Lisa nodded her head, but still couldn't speak. Her brain was completely engulfed in the trauma that had just happened to her.

"You have a brother who escaped?" Lisa asked.

The young girl nodded her head again. That gave Lisa some hope. Perhaps this young brother was able to get some help.

Once the Muslim women went outside the tent, Lisa kept fishing for information from the other captive women about them and how long they'd been there.

She learned that most of the women had had husbands who either had been murdered in front of them or had been converted to Islam in an effort to save their lives. The women did not know for sure if their husbands were truly converts or just playing the game, trying to keep both of them from being killed.

"I know my husband is not a Muslim, no matter what he pretends to be. He told me that he would never convert to Islam, but in order to keep us alive he had to pretend. So he has done what he has had to do to keep us both alive," one lady said.

"We may have to do the same thing. I just hope David realizes that and doesn't try to be the hero that I know he wants to be," Lisa said quietly to no one in particular.

The young girl that she held in her arms finally began to calm her crying. She had cried so hard that she had no tears left. Lisa was unsure at this point what had exactly happened, but she was about to find out.

There was a rustling outside of the fence when the tent flap opened and Laura was pushed in and down to the ground, completely naked. Lisa stood up and came towards the front of the cage as the Muslim women used their canes to hit Laura and pushed her into the cage with Lisa and the other girl.

They grabbed Lisa and pulled her out, as they locked Laura and the young girl into the cage.

Lisa began to hit and kick and scream as the women tried to get her to move with them. The women began to beat Lisa until she fell to the ground.

"Why are you American women so stubborn? You will not win this. You must obey," the lead Muslim woman said. They grabbed Lisa and took her into the house to prepare her for Sayid.

Lisa wasn't having it. She did not plan on having anything taken from her unwillingly. She fought the women repeatedly as they tried to get her to comply. But Lisa was strong willed, and had no intention of letting this creep touch her.

"Do you like your slavery? Is that what you really think you should be?" Lisa asked the Muslim women.

As they tried to strip her of her clothes, she continued to pummel and hit them to try to keep them off of her. The head Muslim woman had had enough and pulled out a large bamboo stick that took only three strikes before Lisa was on the floor in pain.

"You will obey. You will do as you're told."

Lisa was curled up into a ball on the floor. The pain forced her to re-evaluate her circumstances. She decided that if they wanted to do anything to her, that she

STRIKE POINT: ADRIFT

would not resist, but she would also not help them. She let her body go limp, and that created much more effort for the women to bathe her and prepare her for Sayid.

It was a bigger struggle for the Muslim women to finish preparing her but once they had, they took her into Sayid's bedroom and put her on the bed.

Lisa cursed and yelled at them repeatedly, regardless of her ability to fight back. She wanted to make sure that she got in every single word before the lead woman finally slapped her so hard across the face that her nose bled.

"This one should be secured. She could be a problem," one of the Muslim women said.

One of the women took out a rope from underneath her robe and began to tie Lisa to the headboard of the bed so she couldn't escape.

"You filthy perverts! No one should be forced to serve another," Lisa yelled as she kicked her feet towards her captors.

Sayid finally entered the room and the women quickly vacated.

"I see I have a wild one," Sayid said with an evil grin.

"Don't you fucking touch me. I'll fucking kill you," Lisa said as she struggled against the ropes.

Sayid let out a loud chuckle as he pounced up on her and straddled her hips, keeping her from being able to kick him.

Lisa fought hard and kept trying to kick him until Sayid grew tired of her fighting. He balled up his fist and punched her in the face.

When Lisa finally came to, she was back in the cage with Laura, her eye swollen shut and blood dried on her face. She felt like she had been in a car accident.

"Lisa, are you okay?" was all Laura could think to

EMERSON HAWK

ask.

"I will slowly remove his dick. Nice and slow and painful," Lisa said, vowing to make it come true.

CHAPTER 17

David and I watched as Lisa was dragged, kicking and screaming into the house. We both knew that Lisa had a strong will and most likely would try to fight her attacker. We could hear the screams coming from inside the house and David winced every time he heard her.

"I'm sorry," was all I could think of to say. There was no comforting either of us in this situation. We were totally helpless and hated that the women that we loved were being beaten and raped. These animals were not fit to live and we wanted to make sure of that.

"I will kill him. It may be the last thing I do, but I will kill him," David said through tightly gritted teeth as his jaw clenched in anger.

"If we can ever get out of here, we will. I promise. I don't think this man or any of these other men should be allowed to live after the atrocities they have committed. How can someone be so cruel to someone who took them in? It just makes no sense," I stated.

David began to pick at the ropes that tied the cage together in an effort to loosen them.

"If you opened that you may fall and kill yourself," I said.

"I know that. But I can't just sit here any longer. I can't let this continue. I have to do something," David replied.

I understood where he was coming from. But I also saw how high up we were, and I knew that if we tried to escape these cages that it most likely would kill us or we would die falling to the ground.

I began to softly pray for intervention and guidance in our current situation. I knew that our situation looked pretty hopeless, that there were very little options without some type of help. Even if David and I could escape, there were just too many of them to try to kill them all. It was so risky, but we were at the point that it could be our only option.

I didn't like the thought of death, but I liked the thought of living under tyrannical rule even less. If I had to die, then so be it. I prayed that we would die in a way that was pleasing to God, but I wasn't exactly sure what that even meant.

David heard me and began to pray as well. We prayed together for our wives who were being brutally abused. We prayed that we would have the good conscience to make the right decisions when the time came.

Our prayers were interrupted by the sound of Lisa screaming and then silence. David gripped the bars of his bamboo hanging cage and tears rolled down his face. He knew what was happening and there was nothing he could do to stop it.

We watched the Muslim women carry Lisa's limp

STRIKE POINT: ADRIFT

body out of the house and back to their tent. David could not hold in his anger any longer.

"You animals will all die. Even if it's not by my hand, you will die by an American," David yelled as the drunken Muslims laughed off his anger.

They had no idea what was in store for them.

CHAPTER 18

David and I were forced to spend the next three days in agony as we were starved and deprived of water. We watched our wives being violated by Sayid and as much as we wanted to rescue them, we had no way out.

On the fourth day, we were lowered to the ground and given a small amount of water. Both David and I were weak from lack of water and food. We were brought into the grassy center and pushed down onto our knees once again.

"Today is your day of decision. You have two choices. You can die or you can become a servant to Allah. As you have seen, those who choose not to serve Allah are given only one option. If you choose to serve Allah, then you will become one of our team as many others before you," Sayid said, his demeanor almost happy.

David and I knew that we had to try to convince him that we would convert. But it had to sound real.

STRIKE POINT: ADRIFT

I wasn't sure he would even believe us. If they were so willing to lie to all Americans in order to take over the country, why would he think that we'd not use the same tactics?

"How will we know if Allah wants us to be his servants?" I asked.

"Oh, so you are actually thinking now, are you?" Sayid inquired.

"Yes, if Allah wants us to be his servants, how will we know?" David repeated.

"First, you must make your proclamation here for everyone to hear and see, that you have chosen to follow the word of Mohammad and the teachings of Islam," Sayid explained.

"Are you ready to proclaim your faith?" he asked.

I nodded. David followed suit.

"Then repeat after me, 'There is no true Deity but Allah, and Muhammad is the Prophet of God.'"

David and I repeated the simple phrase, and I wondered if that was all there was.

"Good! Very good. Now, you will have to pass a test," Sayid continued.

"What kind of test?" I said, barely able to hold myself upright.

"You shall go with your brothers and they will teach you the ways of Islam," Sayid said as we were taken with several men to one of the tents on the edge of camp. There, we were given water and food. The men were now much more friendly.

It was as if someone turned on a switch to their humanity, and they actually cared about what happened to us. It was confusing as hell, but I didn't care at the moment. I was starving and dying of thirst, so all I could think about was getting as much water inside me as I could.

We were given a cot and told we could rest and recuperate overnight, but that until we had passed the test, we would still be under guard.

"What is this test?" I asked one of them, as I pushed the stale bread into my mouth.

"It is the true test of a Muslim. You will be trained to fight, but will also have to do something that will cause you to question your choice. If you make the right decision, you will become a true Muslim. If you fail, then you are considered an enemy and will be killed," he replied.

I nodded and continued eating, occasionally glancing over at David, who was listening but focused on eating and drinking as well.

We hated leaving Lisa and Laura to fend for themselves, but we knew that as long as they complied, they would still be alive. Our plan was to convince the brotherhood that we were going to accept Islam and Allah so that we could use that trust to take them down.

If we could keep up the act, we might actually have a chance at taking these savages down, even if it meant doing it slowly and one at a time.

CHAPTER 19

We were led through the forest to another small clearing that looked like it had been used before. There were only two tents, but there were a couple of stuffed feed bags hanging from the trees.

We were both given a copy of the Quran and told to read it and study it. We were shown how to pray five times a day. We followed suit with the other Muslims, so that they would believe we were being converted.

The first day was spent sitting around, listening to one of them preach.

"I never knew that Allah was so loving and peaceful," I said to one of the Muslim men.

"Yes, my brother. He is wise in his ways. We just need to follow him and he will take us to our eternity when the time comes with many great rewards," he replied.

"I like the sound of that," David said and forced a

smile.

So far so good. If we could keep up the act, we might actually have a chance.

* * *

"There's only five of them. If we plan it right, we can take them out and get back to the girls in a day. I watched where we came from, so I could remember how to get back to them. It is just west of here," David whispered as we lay quietly in our cots.

"Agreed. But we need to find a way to get our hands on a knife or a gun or something. I don't have the strength in my bare hands to kill someone like you do. I don't have that training yet," I said.

"That's okay, I will show you tomorrow. When we're training. I will nod and show you a few moves that they are not showing us. It will be when they break for lunch and leave us to practice. They will be busy eating and not paying attention. That's when I'll show you the moves," David said.

We tried to sleep, but it was difficult. The few nights that we had been out here, were nights away from Lisa and Laura, who were undoubtedly fighting their own battles. As much as we could fake our way through this terrible ordeal, we knew that they did not have that luxury.

I closed my eyes and prayed as often as possible that the girls would be okay. That even though they were being taken against their will, there would be some kind of protection for them to mentally and emotionally deal with it.

The next day went exactly as David had predicted. Around lunch time, the Jihadis decided to take a break

STRIKE POINT: ADRIFT

and they went to sit under a tree while we practiced our moves with sticks. They would not give us any type of real weapons for fear that we would use them on the men. We still had several tests to go through before they would be convinced that we had truly converted.

We kept playing the part and tried to keep the suspicions down.

Once they had all sat down and began to relax and eat, David showed me a few simple moves that would allow me to easily break a neck or deal a blow that would incapacitate someone, if I could get the right angles.

We watched cautiously to make sure that they weren't paying serious attention to what we were doing, as David taught me these moves.

"The move will all depend on where you are in relation to where the enemy is. Most of the moves don't need a lot of strength, but do need accuracy. Try not to think about it, just do it," David explained as he showed me just a few self-defense moves to make sure I didn't get killed in the process.

We had been out in this training area for about four days and began to question how long it would be before we could be considered "qualified" servants of Allah.

The Muslim trainers were overjoyed with our interest in Islam and were happy to share some life experiences they had. We sat around and listened to them as they droned on about their conquests and how they would lie, cheat, and connive their way into any country that they wanted. They bragged about how they would use Islam to infiltrate other countries and take them over with the sheer volume of people.

David and I tried our best to show that we were being compliant and that we wanted to share in their glory and be part of their revolution. But in our minds, we

EMERSON HAWK

were both disgusted and angry that these animals had been allowed to infiltrate our country.

"So, how will we know when we are ready?" David asked the leader of our group.

We were interrupted by the sound of someone approaching. It was two of our group and with them was a young man that had his arms tied behind his back, shirtless.

"It looks like you will have your opportunity tonight," the leader said as they brought the young man into the clearing and pushed him down to his knees.

David and I faked a smile as we realized what we were about to be asked to do. There was no way I was going to comply with this.

CHAPTER 20

The poor young man was crying and shaking as he was brought into the clearing by two of the Jihadi trainers. He was pushed down to his knees.

"This is one of the Christians that need to be eradicated. Tonight, you will have the honor of beheading this man in Allah's name and for Islam," the leader said.

"Allahu Akbar!" the group said collectively and David and I joined in, but looked at each other warily.

My pulse quickened as I thought about how we would have to make this work. There were five men and just two of us. They would be handing one of us a knife to do the beheading, but we would still be one weapon short. The boy was taken and tied up to a tree for the afternoon.

"Has he been given the opportunity to convert to Islam?" I asked the leader.

"Yes, my brother, he has. And he has refused. He has

made his choice," he replied.

I nodded my head and looked down at my feet.

"You seem troubled, my brother," the leader asked me.

"I wonder if I might be allowed to speak with him. I may be able to convince him otherwise. You all have taught me the love of Allah and perhaps as a former Christian, I can speak to him in a language he may understand," I said.

The leader rubbed his chin and furrowed his brow. He looked as if he was contemplating my request.

"So, you think you might be able to change his mind?" he asked me.

"I don't know. We may still have to follow through with Allah's word. Do you think Allah would appreciate another follower?" I asked, hoping that giving the leader the decision would prove fruitful.

Since the leader was an ego-maniac like Sayid, he liked the idea of having the chance to have another convert under his belt. I imagined it gave him the sense of the power he craved.

"I think you might try, my brother. But if he refuses, then we have no other options. You do understand, correct?" he said.

I nodded my head and said, "I agree, praise be to Allah."

I glanced at David briefly as I walked over to the young man and sat down next to him. He was deep in prayer and I reached out my hand to touch his shoulder, startling him. I kept my back towards everyone, so that they couldn't see or hear my words.

"What's your name, son?" I asked.

"Sam. Sam Frost."

"Listen to me very carefully. I can only say this once.

STRIKE POINT: ADRIFT

Nod if you understand me." He nodded.

I carefully contemplated my words. For a brief moment, I worried that this might be a trick of some kind. That this boy was brought to test us to see if we were truly becoming converts and would follow through with what was expected of us, or if we would try to use the situation to get the upper hand. I had to take the chance that this was legit and that this boy really wasn't a Muslim test.

"We have a plan to free you, but you have to follow along. It will be scary. But you have to listen and follow the plan, so that we can get all of us out of here safely. Do you understand?" I asked.

Again he nodded, but he looked like he was having a hard time comprehending what I was saying, and I wanted to make sure that he did not slip up from the plan.

"I've told them that I've come over to convince you to convert to Islam. But that is not why I'm really here. No matter what happens, I will not hurt you. But we need to pretend as if we are going to."

"Okay..." His voice cracked.

"When they hand me the knife tonight, instead of using it on you, I will push you down on the ground and use the knife on one of the Jihadis instead," I explained.

His eyes got wide as he realized what I was saying to him. He had been trying to come to grips with being killed, but now he had hope. He still needed to play along and there was no guarantee that he wouldn't get hurt. There was no guarantee that this plan would even work and we all could wind up dead, but this was the best chance we had at the moment.

I explained the rest of the plans to him, but the only way this would work was if he pretended to refuse.

EMERSON HAWK

"Okay, so now I want you to begin cussing me out and yelling at me. Make it believable. They need to think you are refusing Islam."

The boy began to yell and cuss, spitting at me and calling me a traitor. He managed to do a good job of making it believable.

I walked back over to the lead Jihadi and shook my head. "It appears he wants to die tonight. It's too bad, he would have been a good asset to Islam."

He reached out and put his hand on my shoulder. "You tried, my brother, that is all you can do. Either Allah is in one's heart or not. After dinner, we will send him to his God."

I nodded and forced a smile.

Now, all we had to do was make sure that the trainers were standing close enough to follow through with our plan.

The afternoon was spent praying and reading the Quran before dinner, then we lit a fire for our last night of training. When the time came, the young boy was brought forward and placed on his knees before us.

"And which one of you shall send this man to his God?" the lead Jihadi asked.

I stood up and claimed the task. "I will do it. I am ready to serve Allah. It is my duty."

It was so hard for me to say those words. It made my stomach sick and I almost lost my dinner, but I knew I had to complete this task in order for us to escape. There was no turning back at this point.

David had shown me several moves that I'd practiced only a few times in the days prior. I was scared to death that I would not be able to follow through, but this was our last chance. We knew that this was the only opportunity we would have.

STRIKE POINT: ADRIFT

As we gathered around the fire, one of the Jihadi stood next to me with a very large knife, calling me over to stand behind the boy, who was reciting the Lord's Prayer softly as tears rolled down his face. No doubt he was afraid, and worried that we wouldn't be able to follow through with what I'd told him.

He continued to pray to God as the entire group began to chant 'Allahu Akbar'. The leader of the group began to quote verses from the Quran about how it was our duty to eradicate all infidels that didn't follow Islam and that by me performing this eradication, it would guarantee me a place at the right hand of Allah.

The Jihadi standing next to me handed me the knife. I looked over at David who was readying himself for his next move. There would be three shouts of 'Allah Akbar' and then, I was supposed to start beheading this boy. On the second shout, I pushed the boy face down onto the ground and quickly turned, using the knife to go up into the bottom jaw of the Jihadi standing behind me, burying it to the hilt.

The man dropped to the ground and blood spurted everywhere as he held his throat.

At this point, I wasn't thinking but just reacting. A second Jihadi began running towards me. As he got closer, I slid into home plate flipping him on to his back as I turned and came down with the knife right into his chest.

Looking over to David, he had managed to take out one Jihadi with a quick flick and broke his neck, but was immediately pinned down by the other one who had a knife to his throat.

I ran as fast as I could towards them, but before I could get there, the fifth Jihadi took his machete and drove it through the back of the man who was attacking

David, surprising us all.

David quickly pushed the dying man off and took his knife, raising it high above the man who had just used the machete on his comrade.

"I'm Christian! I'm not a Muslim! Please, don't kill me!" the man said, as he dropped to his knees and begged for his life.

David and I had moved so quickly that we didn't realize just how fast we had dropped four of the five men. The young boy was on his feet and had used one of the dead Jihadis knives to cut himself free of the ropes.

"How do we know you're not lying? How do we know you're telling the truth?" David asked, still shaking from his near death experience.

"My name is Alex. I am in the same situation as you. I was just trying to stay alive and had no skills other than what they taught me here. So I had to do what was necessary to stay alive. But I am not a convert. I am a Christian," he said as his hands were still raised above his head.

David and I stood upright and caught our breath. We realized that this poor guy had probably been pulled into the web of deceit for quite some time before we had arrived. He was coping with his situation the best way that he knew how.

"Okay, if you are telling the truth, then how many of them are left back at camp and how many others are also Christians pretending to be Muslims?" David asked, reaching out a hand to the man to help him to his feet.

"I'm not sure of either. They keep us moving around so much, it makes it hard to know who is truly a Muslim and who is faking it," he replied.

"So what did they have you do to prove you were a Muslim? Who did you have to kill to be accepted?" I

STRIKE POINT: ADRIFT

asked.

"I saw this coming. A year ago, my wife and I began to learn about Islam because there were so many coming into town. At first, we were open to accepting them, like so many others." Alex's eyes began to fill with tears.

"Then, I began to hear things about them. Like how they will appear to integrate by lying or anything else, but that their true purpose was to take over the country and turn it into an Islamic State. So I bought a Quran to try to understand the truth. I know how the Bible can be misinterpreted and I thought this was the same thing."

Alex sat down on a stump and put his hands over his face, trying not to show his built up pain.

"I thought people were just being bigoted and racist, until I read it for myself. I saw the truth. I saw that what I was hearing was exactly what was happening, and it scared me. I tried to talk to others about it, but they wouldn't listen. So my wife and I decided to get familiar with customs, in case we needed to pass ourselves off as Muslim. That's how I ended up here. She's one of the women back at camp," he said, trying to maintain his composure.

David and I had to figure out how to use this to our advantage. If he was pretending, then there were probably others that were as well. If we went in and began just killing everyone, we might be killing the wrong people.

"They're expecting us to return tonight. They had the boy in a different location, waiting to be used for this purpose. We were all supposed to return with the boy's head to prove that you had converted," Alex explained.

"Yeah, and they're also expecting us to return with four other Muslims."

CHAPTER 21

"Here, take this and eat it quickly," one Muslim woman said as she pulled out several apples from underneath her gown and tossed them to everyone. "Eat quickly and bury any remains of your food so that it is not discovered."

"Who are you?" Laura asked as she bit quickly into the apple.

"My name is Sadie and I am not a Muslim. I am a Christian, but we have had to pretend so that we could stay alive. My husband is one of the men that is with your husbands," Sadie replied.

"Is he a convert?" Lisa asked.

Sadie shook her head no. "We knew that this type of thing was coming and we prepared ourselves so that we could appear to be Muslim when necessary," Sadie said as she continued to give apples to the rest of the girls.

She then went over to the table and took out several cups of water to give all of them to drink. They were

STRIKE POINT: ADRIFT

so thirsty and hungry that they were quite weak at this point. After several days of being locked up in a cage in the heat with very little water, they'd had little energy to resist any advances from their captors.

"I have an idea, but I need to make sure that you're willing to go through with it. You have to be willing to kill in order for it to work," Sadie said.

"Oh, I have no problems killing these savages," Lisa replied.

Laura pondered it for a moment, then nodded her head. "If I have to, I will. If it will keep us alive, then I'll do whatever it takes."

Sadie looked around at the other women who all were nodding yes as well.

"Good. Then here's what we'll do. When I come to get one of you later, there will be only one other woman with me. Once I unlock the cage, you and I can take her down. Once she is taken down, we can use her clothing to fake getting another one of you out and taking you inside. We must make sure that she is dead and we can put her in the cage. Since the men never come inside here, they will not know that she is missing because they do not pay attention to most of the Muslim women, now that you're here," Sadie explained.

Laura and Lisa agreed that it was risky, but they were willing to take the chance.

"What about Jenny? Where's Jenny?" Laura asked. She had been taken the day after her parents had been beheaded and not seen since.

Sadie looked down at the ground sadly. "Jenny is in the basement. I don't know if she's even still alive. I have not been allowed to go down there."

Lisa shook her head in disgust. "These people are not human. They are savages. How could this have happened?"

"It's been going on for quite a long time. My husband and I saw it a year ago. We knew that something big was coming, but we did not know how to stop it. We tried talking to people, but no one would listen. People pouring over the border and no one knows where they ended up. It was the perfect way for us to be infiltrated and taken over," Sadie replied.

"But why did our government allow it to happen?" Laura asked.

"Your guess is as good as mine. There are all kinds of speculations but…" Sadie stopped mid-sentence as we heard some of the men walking by.

"Listen, we can talk more later. I need to go before they get suspicious." Sadie gave the girls more water before taking the bucket out to refill it.

"If we can do what she says, there's a chance we can all escape. We have to be aware and ready to go at a moment's notice." Lisa said as she looked at the gaunt faces of the other women. They were all weak and she wasn't sure if any of them would make it out alive. Laura and Lisa had been quite well fed up until a few days ago, so they still had quite a bit of strength left despite being severely dehydrated.

Later that evening, Sadie returned with one other woman. She gave Lisa a nod as she went to unlock the cage. The woman grabbed Lisa and began to drag her out when Sadie took a rope that she'd had under her gown and pulled it out, wrapping it twice around the woman's neck and pulling tight. Lisa grabbed the woman's throat and began to squeeze hard as both of them choked the life out of the woman. They watched as her eyes rolled back into her head and she went limp, dropping to the ground.

STRIKE POINT: ADRIFT

Lisa stood back and Sadie dropped to her knees in exhaustion as they saw what they had done. The adrenaline was the only thing keeping them alive.

"Quickly, get her gown off and put it on Laura," Sadie said, as she went over and unlocked the other girls' cages. Lisa was shaking, but she knew that this was her only way out. Laura put on the gown and covered her head and face with the veil.

"We will take Lisa inside and there, we can get her another gown. They will not suspect two of us coming back out and we will bring more gowns for you. You need to stay here until we come back out. Do not try to leave just yet. If they see you, you will be killed. It's almost dark and you need the night to be able to escape," Sadie explained.

They took the dead woman's body and placed her inside the cage that Lisa and Laura had previously occupied. Then, they took Lisa into the house without anyone taking notice.

Making their way up and into the bathroom, they closed the door behind them and all let out the collective breath they'd been holding.

"Now what?" Laura whispered.

"Be ready. I'll call Nina to come and assist. When she arrives, you both will have to help me take her down. She is strong and always carries that damn cane," Sadie said.

Nina was the head Muslim woman that had given everyone else direction. She was also the meanest and most brutal.

"Here, take this rope and wrap it around your wrists so that it looks like you are tied up. Then use it around her neck when she enters. Laura, grab a towel to put over her face. If we can get her down on the floor, we can do this. Are you ready?" Sadie asked.

Laura and Lisa both nodded and got into position. Lisa was in front of the door and Laura took a place behind the door.

Sadie went down the hall and told Nina that she needed help. As Nina opened the door, she saw Lisa standing there.

"Oh, it's the trouble-maker," Nina said. It would be her last words.

As Sadie shut the door, the three women made quick work of Nina. Lisa used the rope around her neck and Laura covered her face to help suffocate her. She was down within a minute.

The three women sat on the floor, looking at Nina. Even though these women were Muslim, they couldn't help but feel bad for them for being brainwashed into thinking they were doing something good by torturing other people.

"C'mon, let's get her undressed and put her body in the tub. The shower curtain will keep her hidden. None of the men come in here anyway." Sadie said.

When they undressed Nina, they found a knife in a sheath strapped to her leg.

"This will come in handy," Lisa said as she strapped it to her own thigh.

As they finished putting the gown on Lisa, they heard gunshots. They all instinctively dropped to the floor before Laura peeked her head over the window sill to see if she could find out what was going on.

Even in the darkness, she knew her husband's figure.

CHAPTER 22

"How many Christians are still there? And how many men in total?" David asked Alex.

"There are thirty-seven men in total. I only know of two Christians for sure. That doesn't mean there aren't more, but I can only vouch for two. And it's only because they were two of the people that listened to me during the past year and took my advice to educate themselves on pretending to be Muslims," Alex replied.

"Okay, well unfortunately, if we can't get them out of the camp before we start taking them down, they may be killed." David said.

Alex nodded his head. He knew that it was a chance they would have to take to try to free the women.

"If we go in from the east side, that's where one of the two men I know of sleeps. He might be inside and if he is, we can pull him to safety," Alex said.

"Are we sure we want to risk that? If we are caught trying to rescue the two men that you are speaking of, then we have lost our chance at taking down the other men," I said.

"John is right. It's too risky. What we need to do, is first take out the men who are guarding the perimeter. We can do that quietly and as we take them down, we will then have a better chance at getting your friends out," David said.

Alex nodded. He knew that David was right and it was better for them to try to take out the guards that were walking the perimeter one at a time.

"There is one spot that is easy to watch the camp and not be seen. It's over near the river's edge, where the tree line and brush is pretty thick, but it also has a lot of thorns," Alex said.

David thought about it for a minute. "Let's head over there now. We need to make sure they can't see us."

As we quietly made our way back towards the camp, Alex led us over to the area that allowed us to see what was going on and not be detected. We stood quietly and monitored how many men were there and how they slowly walked around. It looked like there were only about ten men that circled the perimeter and they all kept the same pace.

We all ducked down and decided that David would be the best one to take the men down. He had the training to be stealthy and knew how to take a man down quietly.

The only other option was for Alex or I to draw attention to us from one of the guards and then take him down as he got closer. That was a more dangerous option.

"Let me first see how hard this will be. When were they expecting us to return?" David asked. Alex looked up at the sky before looking back at David. "They are expecting us now. The time was set for sunset and once that was done, we were to return to camp so that as it got dark, we would all celebrate your conversion. If we delay much longer, they might get suspicious," Alex replied.

"Then we need to get on with it. We need to start taking these men out so that there are less of them to fight. I just wish I knew these woods better. I can't see shit out here and I don't know the terrain," David said.

David scanned the tree line to locate the best place to take down the guards. On the back of the camp, there was a wide oak tree that the guards would walk past that would allow David to remain hidden, if he stood in the shadows. He readied one of the knives as he made his way over to the oak and hid in its shadow.

Waiting until one of the men walked by, David made his move. In one swift action, he walked up behind the Jihadi and quickly snapped his neck with a quick spin. The man dropped to the ground and David dragged him into the forest, relieving him of his weapon.

I made myself as small as possible a few trees behind David, in case he needed my help. As he would drag the guard into the trees, I helped to pull the dead man deeper in, so he would not be seen.

David managed to pick off four more men before they noticed something was up. With their suspicion raised, David and I took the weapons and began to head back over to where Alex was.

As we got closer to the brush where Alex had been hiding, we saw two men next to him. David and I ducked behind a couple of trees, waiting to see what happened.

They had Alex down on his knees and we heard one of the guards mumbling something in Arabic. There was a glow of a torch and we saw another man approach with Sayid. We couldn't make out what they were saying, but we knew what was going to happen as soon as Sayid pulled his pistol.

David and I both winced as we watched Alex's body drop to the ground, the result of the bullet passing through his brain from Sayid's gun.

I closed my eyes and prayed for him. Not knowing if my prayers were even being heard. David motioned to me to retreat back into the forest, but as we turned around, we were both met with rifles in our faces.

CHAPTER 23

"It was nice knowing you, David," I said, as I watched the sunrise from my hanging bamboo cage.

This had not been the first time I had been facing death since the blackout. But the type of death coming was something that was scary in ways that you can only imagine in those darkest dreams you want to forget.

I knew beheadings were the preferred way of the Jihadis. And there was a time that I'd never understood how someone could not be haunted by killing so many people, and in the manner in which these people did.

But I was beginning to understand. After knowing what Sayid and his men were doing to the women in the camp, it was easy for me to envision some of the horrible things I might wish on them.

I prayed for forgiveness for those thoughts. While I do believe in an eye for an eye, and I am not opposed to the death penalty, I don't believe that torture is right under any circumstances. I knew David probably dis-

EMERSON HAWK

agreed with me on that point. He had seen combat and had no problems dishing out pain to those who would do us harm.

I guess my lack of exposure to those hard choices made me soft, and that was something I would have to live and die with.

"It was nice knowing you too, John. I wished it would have been longer. I really wanted you and Laura to meet my family. And I was hoping that maybe you'd be godparents to kids that Lisa and I might've had," David replied, his voice shaking with the thoughts of what he would never see.

"How did we get here? How did we come so far as a country, only to be pushed back into the dark ages with an enemy in our house? It just makes me angry and confused," I said.

"I know. Me too. And what's worse, is that it could have been avoided. I mean, I think it could have. I dunno anymore. When I think back to everything I've learned about how our government has deceived the people and the military, it just makes my blood boil. Believe me, most of the military have been misled on so many things. Or only told what they needed to get a job done. It's like our government didn't care at all about us. We were just here to do their dirty work," David steamed.

"Would there have been anything you could have done about it? I mean, even if you knew then what you know now…would there have been anything that you personally could have done to change things? As big as this is?" I asked.

I watched David as he pondered the question, a pained look on his face.

"Of course. I mean, when I began to see things deteriorating a few years ago, I told my family that they needed to prepare. That something was coming, but that I wasn't sure how or when or where, but that they needed to make sure they had certain things in place."

"Did they listen?" I asked.

"Yes, for the most part. My mother thought I was overreacting, but dad knew I was serious. He sensed that something was coming anyway. He'd been watching the invasion into our town and seeing things change. At first, it wasn't a big deal. But when Obama got elected and basically admitted he was a Muslim, that did it for him. He's been prepping ever since," David replied.

"I hope they are doing okay. I hope they will manage to make it through all this. I still have no idea if any of my family are still alive. Guess I'll never know." The sadness became overwhelming as the tears pricked at my eyes.

My sadness turned to outrage when I saw Laura and Lisa being dragged out of the house and held at gunpoint, down in the grassy circle. I knew it was time. They were planning on making a spectacle of out of us to all of the other members. Making sure that everyone knew what would happen to those who tried to deceive them.

Laura and Lisa were wearing the dresses of the Muslim women. I can only guess that they were trying to find a way to escape. Perhaps if David and I hadn't messed it up, they would have. Now, we'd never know.

Both women were sobbing as they were pushed down to their knees. David and I both gritted our teeth in anger as they lowered our cages to the ground, bringing us out, one by one.

My instinct was to take my chances running away in the hopes that I would be shot instead of beheaded, but we had been warned the night before that if we tried, then the women would be tortured for weeks on end until they died. Neither one of us were willing to risk it. We already knew these people were savages and even if we were dead and it didn't matter to us anymore, we knew they would carry through with the threat.

So we didn't. We obeyed their instructions. The last thing either of us wanted was a slow and painful death for anyone.

David and I were pushed down to our knees, opposite of the women. They wanted to make sure we'd see each other die.

Seeing Laura cry was the one thing that would always make me lose my mind. Even those times when she would cry for those little things that women would cry for. Any time she hurt, it made my heart break. Today was no exception.

She mouthed the words 'I love you' as best she could. I replied in equal silence. I longed to hold her one last time.

Sayid stepped out of the house and began to preach some bullshit about Allah. I couldn't hear him. My mind and heart were intently focused on Laura, who was shaking uncontrollably.

I glanced briefly over at Lisa and David, who were having the same conversation with each other. Their eyes were showing that they loved each other, and their bodies trying to deal with the stress of what was about to come.

I steeled myself as best I could, and began to softly speak The Lord's Prayer. Laura heard me and followed my lead, as did David and Lisa.

Sayid was enraged by this defiance and us interrupting his preaching about Islam being the "religion of peace".

I knew that it would bring an end to our lives sooner than later, but we all began to pray in unison, our voices getting louder and carrying over the voice of Sayid.

STRIKE POINT: ADRIFT

Sayid had finally had enough, and raised his hands to signal to those that held the knives to our throats.

"Close your eyes, Laura," I said out loud. I didn't want her last vision to be of all of us being beheaded.

I nodded one last time towards Laura and closed my eyes. He might be able to take our lives, but I wasn't going to see my own wife beheaded in front of me before my own death.

I held my breath, waiting for the cold steel to begin its journey through my flesh, when I heard the sound of gunshots, and felt the man holding me let go.

As I opened my eyes, Sayid was running for the trees and the four men who had been holding knives at our throats were all dead, a gunshot to each of their heads.

CHAPTER 24

"Get down!" David yelled as the four of them all fell down to the ground, trying to avoid the gunfire that ensued.

David was the first to retrieve one of the knives, releasing his own ropes, then John's. They both went over and released their wives, hugging them briefly before they began to pick up weapons to take off after the remaining Jihadis.

"Who's helping us?" John asked David.

"I don't know, nor do I care, let's finish this!" David said, as he began seeking out all of the Muslim men and women that were still alive.

"Go inside and kill any of the women who are left. No mercy. They didn't show any to you. Make it quick and thorough," John said to Laura and Lisa as they took the knives from the dead men next to them.

Both women nodded and made their way into the house. They had already taken out a few of the women

STRIKE POINT: ADRIFT

previously and there were only a couple left to handle. Since they were still dressed in the Muslim dresses, they wrapped their heads so they couldn't be recognized.

Laura led the way and Lisa followed as they crept up the stairs and into the rooms where the women were hiding. Laura found both the Muslim women and pretended to be there to help them. She waved for them to come towards her, but as they stood up, both she and Lisa took their knives and went up through the women's abdomens and into their hearts.

As the two women dropped to the floor, the blood began to flood out from underneath them. Laura began crying at the thought of killing. She hated having to hurt anyone. It just wasn't in her nature to be cruel, even to those who were cruel to her.

Lisa wasn't affected in the same way. She wasn't fazed by it and wiped the blood off of the knife on the back of the woman's headdress.

"Look, you have to stop thinking of them as human. It's how I cope. Stop thinking about it. It's all about survival now. That's all that matters," Lisa said, trying to reassure Laura that she wasn't killing for the wrong reasons.

"How can you say that? They were human," Laura said, as she wiped the tears from her face, her knees going weak as she made her way into the hall and slid down the wall to the floor.

"Because people who truly care about others don't hurt them. I'm not saying Americans are saints because we aren't. I know I've read in my history classes about how people have been treated throughout the centuries, even in our own country. But we have evolved. We, as a species, should be beyond killing each other. As you can see, that hasn't happened. So essentially, we are all savages and the thin thread that holds us together disappears as soon as things get tough, or someone doesn't agree with someone else's opinion."

Laura wasn't sure if Lisa was trying to convince her or trying to convince herself. It didn't matter. What mattered was that things had devolved into people killing others because of their beliefs. That wasn't what made America great. What made America the coveted place to be was the fact that you could live here without fear of persecution, as long as your beliefs didn't interfere with someone else's.

"We need to get Jenny. I think she's in the basement, if she's still alive," Laura said.

Lisa held out her hand to Laura and helped her back to her feet. They went through the house to make sure no one else was inside. The gunfire continued outside and sounded like it was being pushed farther and farther away from the house.

Lisa led the way down into the basement. It was dark and musty, and she grabbed a flashlight that was sitting on the stairs.

"Jenny? Honey, are you down here?" Laura called out, hoping that she wouldn't be afraid and unsure if there was anyone else down with her.

Lisa and Laura made their way to the bottom of the steps and shined the light around the room. The windows had been covered over so no light could get through. As they made their way past old antiques, Laura saw her.

She was curled up into a ball onto an old mattress with no sheets. She didn't look alive.

Laura rushed over to her and lifted her up, hoping to find a pulse. It was weak, but she was still alive.

They could both tell that she had been repeatedly

STRIKE POINT: ADRIFT

abused and raped. Laura wondered if Jenny would ever be able to recover. Regardless, they were going to get her out of this place.

"Careful, honey. I got you. We're getting you out of here," Laura said, assuring Jenny that she wouldn't be harmed any longer.

They carried her upstairs and laid her on the couch, covering her naked body with a blanket.

"Get some water. She probably hasn't been fed since she's been here," Laura said as Lisa rushed into the kitchen, returning with a glass for her.

Laura carefully held the water to the girl's mouth. Jenny could barely move, but she took a swallow. Little by little, Laura kept giving her water as long as she could swallow it. Within a few minutes, Jenny began to show a little more life. Both the women were hopeful that it wasn't too late and that Jenny could be saved. She needed medical attention.

Lisa went into the kitchen and found a couple of oranges that she cut into slices. Laura carefully rubbed the orange across Jenny's lips. Jenny pursed her lips on the orange and licked them. That was all she had the energy for.

Little by little, Jenny used her lips to squeeze the juice from the orange into her mouth. Laura took the slice and gave it a little squeeze, allowing the juice to flow into Jenny's waiting mouth. Lisa looked Jenny over and could see the insane bruising all over the child's body.

"You think killing them is harsh. I think it is merciful after seeing what they've done and allowed to happen to Jenny," Lisa said harshly.

Laura understood, and as she looked over Jenny, her guilt faded away.

CHAPTER 25

I told the girls to go inside and take care of anyone in there. They'll be okay," I said to David, who nodded after I'd caught up with him.

"These bastards have scattered. We need to hunt them down and kill all of them. We have no way of knowing who is who, except by the way they're dressed," David said.

"What about the Christians that are here?" I asked quietly, staying low to the ground and leaning next to a tree.

"It's unfortunate, but we'll have to shoot first and ask questions later," he replied.

I nodded my head, not wanting to think about killing one of our own, but there was no way for me to tell if someone was being truthful or not. I looked around and could see men in military uniforms, racing through the forest after the Jihadis.

Most of my fear had subsided now, and all that was

left was an anger I'd never felt before. My need to see all of these abusers dead was unmistakable. I could see now, how easily it was to hate people who had done you wrong. It made killing them easy and unquestionable. A part of me hated that feeling. But another part knew it was necessary to deal with what I was doing.

David and I made our way through some of the trees, until we came upon two of the Jihadis lying down in the brush. David motioned to me and I nodded back as I made my way behind them and hid behind a tree and he took the front.

David steadied himself with his rifle and took a shot, blowing right through the skull of one of the men, splattering brain matter all over his buddy.

The second guy jumped up and began to run towards my direction, and right into the waiting knife I held tightly in my hand. Just like that, two more monsters were gone.

The gunfire finally died down and we laid low, waiting to see if we could find any more immigrants. I peeked around the tree only to see a face I didn't expect. It was General Knox.

David rose from his hiding spot and saluted Knox as I came out from behind my tree, stretching my back from being seated wrong. Making my way over to Knox, I reached out and shook his hand.

"You have no idea how glad I am to see you," I said, smiling.

"Yeah, I'll bet I do. I've been in a similar situation as you boys were tonight. Only it was in 'Nam," Knox replied.

"How did you know we were here?" David asked.

That hadn't occurred to me because I was just relieved that they were there.

EMERSON HAWK

"There was a young boy who went to Washington and told them that his parents' house had been taken over. They all ran away, but he thought his sister and parents had been caught."

David and I looked at each other and grimaced before telling Knox the horrible truth about the family.

"His sister may still be alive, but both his parents were beheaded," David explained.

Knox scowled and shook his head. "Fucking savages. Where's the girl?"

"If she's still alive, back at the house. Laura and Lisa hopefully have her, but she probably needs a doctor," I said.

"We'll take her back with us. If she has the will to live, we'll do our best to heal her," Knox said as he went to help David lift the dead Jihadi and carry him out of the woods.

"Why don't we just leave them here? The animals will make good use of them," I asked.

"We need to keep track of how many are here and how many we dispatch. Since Obama had the border patrol stand down when allowing in all the refugees, no one really knows how many crossed the border. One of our orders is to start keeping track."

"Dispatch?" I asked.

David leaned in and said, "Kill."

We brought out all the dead Jihadis and eventually made our way back into the house where we found Laura and Lisa trying to keep Jenny from dying. Knox brought in a couple of nurses who began to give her an IV drip of saline to rehydrate her little body.

Knox patted Laura on the shoulder. "Don't worry. She'll be okay. Her brother is back at the camp and he will help her cope."

STRIKE POINT: ADRIFT

Laura's eyes filled with tears and I knew she was worried about Jenny, but the nurses would make sure she made it alright.

Laura watched as they carefully carried Jenny to the Jeep, taking off towards town. She turned around and flung her arms around Knox, almost knocking him off his feet.

"Thank you," was all that she could say as she pulled away, leaving Knox blushing.

She then wrapped her arms around me, holding me so tight I almost couldn't breathe. My arms automatically slipped around her waist, pulling her into me. I never wanted to let her go.

Knox waited for a few minutes for all of us to hug each other before speaking.

"There are new orders in place. We have been instructed to eradicate the Muslims. They have proven to us that they refuse to integrate and are not a peaceful people but instead, have waited until they thought they could install Sharia Law and turn America into an Islamic country. We aren't going to let that happen."

"How are you planning on eradicating them?" I asked.

"They will either be shipped back to their country or dispatched," Knox replied.

"That seems kinda harsh. Just killing people because of their beliefs?"

Knox pursed his lips and furrowed his brow.

"A few hours ago, you were down on your knees with a blade pushed up to your throat and your head about to be removed from your body. Why do you think they were going to behead you? Did you do something to them? What about the people who owned this house and took in the refugees, trying to do the right thing?

EMERSON HAWK

Why are these people killing us? Because we don't believe what they believe. Just killing people because of their beliefs."

Laura shrunk back a bit, realizing that he was right. I knew she was troubled and I understood it completely. But in this new world, there was only one way to survive.

Dispatch.

CHAPTER 26

"I'm so sorry," Laura said, and she held Sadie while she cried.

"We did what we thought was right," Sadie replied tearfully. "We tried to be good Americans. But Alex knew things were going to get bad. He always told me that he could die anytime. We'd just come so far. We were so close to making it out together."

We found the two other Christian men in the tent with their wives. They had removed their Muslim clothing, so that no one would confuse them and all of them had stayed low to the ground until the gunfire had stopped.

Our guys broke out the women from the cages and brought all of them into the house to find something for them to wear. They were emaciated but alive and I knew they would recover.

"Sadie, these men will take you into the camp at Washington. There are a lot of really nice people that will help you," Lisa said, patting Sadie on the shoulder.

Sadie and the rest of the women made their way out to the additional Jeeps that had arrived to take them into town, along with their husbands.

"They should be able to give you quite a bit of intel," David said to Knox.

"I hope so. The more we know about how these sleeper cells are situated, the better. What about you guys? You coming back to the camp?"

David and I looked at each other. I knew what he was thinking, but I wasn't sure if the girls were up to continuing without a night's rest and some food.

"I think we'll let the women decide," I said, looking over to Laura and Lisa. They'd had such a rough few days and we all could use a rest.

"I need a day. I need to get some rest and some food. We'll be traveling by foot, yes?" Laura asked.

I nodded and knew we were heading back to camp. It would be better anyway because we could sit down with Knox and tell him what we'd learned. And I knew he wanted to really grill David about anything and everything we'd heard.

The sun was up and we were finally seeing the bloodbath.

With the help of the other men, we gathered up all the bodies and brought them out to where the bonfire pit was. It was hard to see the carnage of what had taken place. I only could imagine what many of these men had witnessed in wars and it gave me a new awareness and appreciation for anyone who had seen combat.

The kind of things I was feeling and experiencing weren't something I was used to, but I knew as we continued our journey home that this might become more common. I could see how easily it was to have PTSD

STRIKE POINT: ADRIFT

and how the brain would keep replaying the bad scenes over and over in my head. If I didn't have my wits about me, I could have curled up into a hole and just wished the world would leave me alone.

But that wasn't the world we lived in anymore. We lived in this new world, that was only going to get harder as we went along.

I watched as one of the men took a photo of each of the dead men's faces. Some of them only had half a face, but he took the photo anyway. It was gruesome at best.

The bodies were all piled up and a small amount of fuel was used to light the flame. Everyone stood upwind as the black smoke began to rise, darkening the sky.

"How many people were here?" Knox asked.

"Thirty-five, I think. Alex said there were thirty-seven total, but two were Christians like him, pretending to be Muslim," David replied.

Knox nodded, "There are only thirty-two bodies. That means three got away."

"One would be Sayid. He was the first one to run into the woods when the shots started," I said, David nodded in agreement.

"Well, they'll probably find another Muslim group to integrate with. There's no point trying to hunt just the three of them down at this point. Of course, I don't have to tell you what to do if you come across them again," Knox said.

David and I both nodded and said in unison, "Dispatch."

Knox nodded before he turned back to the burning pile of bodies.

"Never thought I'd see the day we were doing this here. Not on American soil." Knox shook his head as he began to round up his men.

EMERSON HAWK

He had a few men stay back and watch the fire to make sure it didn't spread, and clean up inside the house as much as they could. He said that he wanted to try to leave the place as clean as possible, in case someone needed it later for a place to stay. He told his men to make sure any blood was cleaned up and anything that was remotely Muslim was burned.

With the body count, it would probably take several days for the pile to be nothing but ash. But when they were done, it was to be covered up so no visible remains were left.

We made our way over to the remaining Jeep and headed back towards Washington. The warm breeze felt good on my skin as I reached over and took Laura's hand. I could see she was far away in thought, probably trying to forget about everything that happened. This was something you couldn't forget. Ever.

"The ladies at the bed and breakfast will give you all rooms and you can get clothes and get cleaned up. I'm sure you'll want to try to sleep if you can. David, when you are ready, I'd like to see you privately," Knox said.

The front porch of the bed and breakfast was welcoming and we needed it now more than ever. We had lost all of our things, so the ladies managed to find some clean clothing from their basement.

"Here you go. I know it isn't perfect, but it should fit and it's clean," said our hostess.

Laura took the clothes and closed the door. She laid the clothes on the bed, but I could tell something wasn't right. She looked at me as she began to stumble. I caught her just before she hit the ground.

CHAPTER 27

"Babe? Babe?" I said, as I held her in my arms. She was awake but incoherent as I tried to get her to respond.

"Help! Get a doctor!" I yelled to anyone who could hear me. The hostess rushed into the room and then ran out to get the doctor.

"Laura? Stay with me. Hang on," I said as I held her in my arms, feeling helpless as to what to do.

She was mumbling something, but I couldn't make out what it was. Just random words that made no sense.

The doctor arrived and began to check her over.

"She's probably dehydrated and faint from lack of food and water. We need to get her hydrated as quickly as possible," he said as he pulled out a saline bag and pushed the needle in her arm.

"We've been seeing a lot of this now. People can only go for a few days without enough water before they become delirious. If that's what it is, this should start to work in a few minutes," he explained, as he stood up and held the bag high so it could get into her system faster.

I watched her as she went in and out of consciousness. I couldn't lose her, not after we'd come so far.

"What if this doesn't help? What if it's something else?" I asked desperately.

"Let's take it one step at a time. You all have been through a lot the last few days. When the body goes through that kind of trauma, it may function for a while but as soon as the threat has passed, it has to catch up. Give this a little time to work and…" the doctor was interrupted by Laura.

"What…happened?" said Laura, looking around the room.

"Oh, thank God. I thought I was going to lose you," I said as I pulled her into me, hugging her.

"She'll be okay. Let this drip finish, then let her drink as much water as she can hold. By morning she'll be back to normal, once she gets enough food and liquid," the doctor reassured me.

"Thanks, Doc," I said as he and everyone else left the room to give us some privacy, knowing full well that there was nothing normal about how we were living.

"How ya feelin?" I asked, brushing the hair away from her face. She tried to push herself upright, but was still too woozy. "Stay down, baby girl. Let that saline get into your system first."

I reached up and grabbed a pillow off the bed for her head, placing it under her.

"Everything just went dark and I couldn't see. Then it felt like I was floating for a minute before Sayid's face showed up. That wasn't fun."

"I'm sorry, love. The Doctor said it's probably due to being dehydrated. After this finishes, you should feel bet-

STRIKE POINT: ADRIFT

ter," I said.

Several minutes later, she was able to sit up without issues. I helped her to her feet and over to sit on the bed.

"If you think you'll be okay, I'm gonna go get something for you to eat," I said as I began to walk towards the door.

"Wait! No don't leave just yet," she said as she began to cry.

I went over and sat down next to her. She was shaking like a leaf. Everything from the past week was probably flooding her brain and creating panic in her mind.

"It's okay, I'm right here. Not going anywhere," I said, as I put my arm around her and pulled her into me.

"How can someone be so horrible? How can humans treat other humans so horrible?" she cried.

"I don't know. Humans are strange creatures for sure. All we can do is try to be the best we can."

"I need a bath. I need to wash the evil off of me."

I nodded and got up and went to the bathroom, starting the water for her to bathe. I kept an eye on her through the crack in the door and could see the stress on her face. All I wanted to do was take the pain away. I just wanted her to feel safe.

After getting the bath ready, I went back into the bedroom and took her hand, gently leading her into the bathroom. I began to undress her when she stopped me.

"No. I need to do this alone. He touched me. He did things…" her voice trailed off.

The sadness and anger that rose up inside me gripped my chest.

"Okay. I'll be right outside if you need me," I said and closed the door as I left the room.

All I could think of right now was hunting down Sayid and killing him. I fantasized about making it slow and painful, making sure to hurt him much more than he hurt Laura or any other woman. I had to shake myself and stop myself from thinking that way. As much as I wanted him dead, that wasn't my way. If I was going to kill him, I just wanted to get it over with, so he couldn't hurt anyone else again.

My emotions wavered back and forth between wanting to cause him pain and trying to rise above that level of hatred.

As I stood looking out the front window, I watched as everyone mingled through the field across the road, working for their supper. I thought about going back to Ben's and maybe that would have been the best thing to do. If we had stayed there, none of this would have happened. At least, not to us.

Then again, how long would it have been before we might have been taken over by a group of Jihadis? I wondered if Ben and George were still safe. I hoped and prayed they were.

The sound of Laura crying pulled me out of my stare as I immediately went to her. Opening the bathroom door, she was sobbing as she sat naked in the tub. I wanted to help, but didn't know how.

As I looked over her body, I could see the bruises from where she'd been beaten. She grabbed the washcloth and tried to cover herself to no avail. But why? I was her husband. She didn't need to hide from me.

But it wasn't me. It was him. He had hurt her in ways I couldn't imagine. I felt the tears welling up in my eyes as I could feel her pain. She drew her legs up and pulled them into her chest, effectively hiding herself.

"What can I do? How can I help?" I asked, feeling more helpless than ever.

She just shook her head and cried, lowering her forehead down onto her knees. I sat down on the commode that was next to the tub, and reached out to stroke her hair. She recoiled, pulling herself away from me. That hurt, but I got it.

I pulled my hand away and got back up to leave. "If you need me for anything, just call. I'll be right out here, babe."

She raised her head up and looked at me squarely in the eyes, her face red and tear streaked. There was a look in her eyes I had never seen before. It was a part of Laura that I had never seen. And when she spoke, it was a different place from within that she was speaking from.

"Kill him."

CHAPTER 28

"Gentlemen, we've been invaded by the devil," General Knox said as he began to share what David and Sadie had shared with him. Sadie wasn't really in a position to teach anyone just yet, but she'd told Knox that after she had some time to heal, she'd be happy to teach what she knew to others to make sure they could protect themselves against being captured and possibly beheaded by the Jihadis.

They were told that they needed to learn the Shahada and learn it in Arabic for it to be believable. They also needed to learn what the five pillars were and which way to face to pray if they had to fake praying to Allah.

With enough knowledge, they'd be able to fool most Muslims into believing they were also Muslim and that might actually keep them alive.

"So what happens if we are pretending to be Muslim, and then we need to prove that we aren't?" one soldier asked.

STRIKE POINT: ADRIFT

"Good question. It's gonna take getting to know them before you can make that determination. In some cases, you may not know and might kill someone who isn't truly a Muslim. But in the world we are in today, it's a chance we'll have to take until we send them back to where they came from," Knox replied.

"So we aren't just going to dispatch them all?" another soldier asked.

"Not unless they force us to. We are still Americans and we don't kill people just for what they believe, even though that's what the Jihadis do. We aren't going to lower ourselves to that level. It's only if our lives are at risk that we would need to take someone out. If they willingly accept deportation, then we will send them home," Knox explained.

There was a buzz about the room as everyone tried to grasp the importance of what was being taught.

"This is just some of the basics. I'll be setting up classes for everyone to attend. It is important that you understand the rules of the Muslim faith to be able to pass yourselves off as one. It is required by everyone who is enlisted, and if the civilians want to attend, we will set up different classes for them," Knox explained.

"Why separate classes?" David asked.

"Because, there are some things that we need to cover that only the enlisted need to know. Even though we are more transparent now than ever to the civilian population, some things still need to be kept secret for our safety and theirs," Knox replied.

David nodded as they finished up their meeting with everyone. It was a good idea and he planned on learning as much as he could before he got back on the road again. He thought about Lisa and hoped she would be okay after everything.

EMERSON HAWK

Before his meeting, he'd made sure she was taken care of. She was so exhausted the day before, from being dehydrated and starved, that all she'd wanted to do was drink until she couldn't stop peeing and eat until she almost threw up.

After filling up with food, she had showered and went to bed, David tucking her in and kissing her on the forehead.

"Would you check on Jenny for me? Would you make sure she made it?" Lisa asked sleepily as her body began to force her down.

"Of course. I need to go take care of some things, but I'll be back later. I love you. We'll get through this."

Lisa reached over and squeezed his hand. "I know. I love you, too."

Fortunately, the small town hospital was nearby. He noticed that there were several horses and buggies that were being used to get through some of the streets. They looked similar to the Amish buggies, but the people driving them weren't dressed in the usual Amish clothing.

He walked up to the main hospital doors and noticed that they were propped open. When he made his way inside, he understood why. Without electricity, there was no air conditioning system to filter the obvious smell of sickness that permeated the corridors. Most hospitals had been built to only use HVAC systems, so none of the windows opened. The smell was almost bad enough to make anyone who came inside sick from the stench.

Despite the smell, everything still appeared to be clean. There was a lady walking down the hall with clean, white folded sheets that she had been taking to the rooms, so someone had to have been washing them.

STRIKE POINT: ADRIFT

"The little girl that was brought in. Her name is Jenny. I need to get an update on her," David said with authority to the nurse.

"Follow me," the nurse said, and she led David into a room near the nurses' station. As he walked in, he could see Jenny lying still under the sheet, her face pale and bruised. An older boy was sleeping in the chair by the window.

"She's been sedated," the nurse whispered. "The doctor thought it was best to help her sleep. She's being given saline to rehydrate her and several vitamin pushes. If she makes it through tonight, she'll probably be… well, she'll live."

David knew what the nurse had meant. Jenny may survive this, but what she had been through would most likely damage her emotionally and mentally for life. Seeing her parents beheaded, and then being repeatedly raped by the animals until she was almost dead, would probably make her wish she hadn't survived.

David's anger against Sayid and the others only grew as he watched the girl struggle to live. The sickness of the teachings of Islam made him wish there was a faster way to rid the world of all of them. To have a so-called 'religion' teach its people that it was okay to abuse children like that was in no way any kind of peaceful religion.

He shook his head as he left the room and he tried to get his anger in check. The nurse followed him out.

"Her brother, Jeremy has been here since she arrived. I don't think she knows he's alive. He'll be here to help her through," the nurse explained as they walked back towards the nurses' station.

"Okay, thank you. I'll probably check back in on her tomorrow," David said as he made his way outside and into the fresh air.

His mind reeled as he thought about what he wanted to do to Sayid if he ever found him. But as he walked past the back of the hospital, he saw several men working on the generator and putting up some salvaged solar panels. It gave him hope that they'd come out of this okay, and people would help others after they'd eradicated the beasts within their borders.

He went back to the bed and breakfast to see if Lisa was awake. He peeked into the room as he tried to be as quiet as possible. Lisa was sitting up in bed with a box of tissues, crying.

"What's the matter, babe?" David said, rushing over to her.

Lisa just shook her head. All that had happened had really gotten to her. She felt guilty about Jenny being the one that'd had to service Sayid.

"I can't stop thinking about Jenny. When she got there, his attention was turned to her and he decided to keep raping her, instead of me and Laura," she explained, "It makes me sick that someone could do that to a little girl. But what's worse is that I know that these animals do it to their own children. Their own daughters and it's accepted as normal. What the hell is wrong with them?"

Lisa sobbed into her tissues as she came to grips with her realizations. David decided against telling her the other horrors that they did to little girls.

He pulled her close and held her, trying to comfort her in the only way he knew how. He took off his boots and got up on the bed next to her, pulling her to him and holding her tight. He stroked his fingers through her hair and wished he could take the pain away. But he knew that it wasn't possible.

STRIKE POINT: ADRIFT

Everyone around him was finally waking up to the truth about the rest of the world and its horrors. The truth about how Islam had been twisted to be used against its own people. And the truth that it had now come to American soil.

As Lisa finally began to calm down, he vowed that he would do everything in his power to stop the continuing invasion. No matter what it took, he wanted his country back. He knew that it would never be like it had been before, but maybe it could be better.

With the right people in charge, and going back to their Constitutional roots, America could one day be great again.

CHAPTER 29

David spent the next day going through the training class on how to fake being a Muslim. It was both eye-opening and enlightening, but angering as he realized the lengths at which they would go to put the Islamic rule into this country.

Like him, most of the men decided that they would prefer to dispatch any Muslims they encountered, but they were ordered to give them the opportunity to be deported instead. David wasn't so sure that he'd follow that order and he knew that most of his comrades probably felt the same way.

John had decided that Laura did not need to take the class. She had been dealing with the trauma of being raped by Sayid and just couldn't handle talking about the Jihadis and their terror tactics. So John decided to take the class on his own, so that he would be aware of anything that he needed to do to protect them. He felt that it would be easier for him to translate the important parts

STRIKE POINT: ADRIFT

back to Laura when the time was right.

Once the classes were over and the girls had had a day to rest and recuperate, they all decided that it was time to move on. Laura didn't really have the desire to continue at all. She wanted to go back to Ben's place instead.

She felt that if they could go back to Ben's, that they would probably have a better chance of surviving for the next several months, instead of trying to make it back to St. Louis. John agreed, but they were over halfway home, so it made sense to try to continue. David also wanted to get to his family's property. Laura reluctantly agreed.

Both Lisa and Laura decided that they wanted to check in on Jenny to see how she was doing before they left. David and John went with them to the hospital to see if she was awake and talking.

"I think it would be best if just the ladies went into the room. She's quite distraught and anyone who is male, other than Jeremy, might trigger her to respond negatively," the nurse explained.

John and David agreed to stay outside and let Lisa and Laura go in to see Jenny. The nurse led them into the room. Jenny was sitting upright in bed, her face still showing quite a bit of bruising from Sayid. Jeremy stood up as they entered the room.

"You must be Jeremy," Laura said.

Jeremy nodded his head. "Yes ma'am," he replied.

"Thank you for telling them to come and rescue us. If you hadn't done so, we'd all be dead," Lisa said as she walked over and gave him a big hug.

Jenny looked up at the two girls as they came and stood by the side of her bed. Laura reached out and gently pushed a strand of her hair behind her ear.

"How are you doing today, honey?" Laura asked.

Jenny looked at them curiously and then over to Jeremy as if she was looking for approval. Jeremy nodded at Jenny.

"I think I'm okay," Jenny said shakily. "I don't remember a lot. I just know that I hurt right now. Like somebody beat me up."

Lisa and Laura looked at each other. Lisa nodded and smiled, "Well, the nurse says you'll be okay. Jeremy will make sure of that. He'll take good care of you."

"Have you seen my parents? I can't imagine where they would've gone. They wouldn't have left me here," Jenny asked.

Laura gave Lisa a look and an almost imperceptible shake. They didn't want to tell Jenny just yet, that her parents were dead and that she'd witnessed it. She was obviously blocking out the crime in her mind.

"Don't worry about that too much. Jeremy will make sure that you get everything that you need. Lisa and I have to leave, but you are in good hands. If you need anything, just let Jeremy or one of the nurses know and they'll take care of it for you. Okay?" Laura said, tears prickling her eyes and threatening to fall.

Jenny nodded as she gave a weak smile.

"You take care of yourself, kiddo. I need to talk to Jeremy for just a few minutes. Is that okay?" Laura asked.

Jenny nodded and Jeremy followed Lisa and Laura out of hospital room into the hallway.

Laura and Lisa pulled Jeremy away from the door, so that their voices couldn't be heard by Jenny. Lisa and Laura looked at each other before they began to speak. They needed to let Jeremy know that his parents would not be arriving and that they were not even sure where their bodies were.

"Jeremy, there's something we need to tell you. And it's not good," Lisa said.

STRIKE POINT: ADRIFT

Before either of the women could say anything, Jeremy interrupted them.

"I already know. David came and talked to me about what happened. He told me that they were beheaded right in front of Jenny. He said that it was quick, but that Jenny saw it all and that it could potentially cause some problems for her later on in life. So I know all about it," Jerry explained with tears welling up in his eyes.

Laura reached out and hugged Jeremy. "I'm so sorry. This should never have happened. Please take care of Jenny, you're all that she has left."

Jeremy nodded his head. "Yes, and she is all that I have, too. But we have the community and I believe that we'll find ways to rebuild and heal."

Laura smiled softly as she pulled away. Then Lisa and Laura left Jenny in the capable hands of her brother.

Several women from the Baptist Church had gathered clothing and supplies for them to take. The people in town were so generous, even though everyone was struggling just to survive themselves. The attitude of the true American had always been to try to help others. This was no different.

They made one last stop to see General Knox before heading out. They knew it was going to be a long walk, but they had all the supplies they would need to make it. Knox said he would have loved to have had extra horses for them to take, but the town just couldn't spare them at the moment.

Horses weren't something that most people had these days. Since everyone used cars, horses were not normally needed for transportation. But the demand for horses was now very high, and the ones that the Amish were allowing everyone to use had to be divvied up to work different areas of land throughout the county.

EMERSON HAWK

"We've loaded you up with what is necessary to get you there. You'll need to probably try to trap some or do a little hunting on the way. If you stay along the river, you'll get there and can use the river for water and fish. There are several life straws that can be used to drink directly from the river without fear of contamination. If you can find a well, that would be preferable, but these will help in case of emergency. Just stay hydrated because if you don't, you'll find yourself weak and not able to keep aware of your surroundings," he cautioned.

"Thank you, sir. And thanks again for coming to save us," David said as he saluted Knox and they all began to make their way down the road.

Before they got too far down the road, Sam came running towards them with a pillowcase tossed over his shoulder.

"Wait! Wait for me!" Sam yelled as they stopped and waited for him to catch up. The group all looked at each other curiously. Had one of them invited Sam and not said anything about it?

"Look, I know that you all are on your way to St. Louis. I want to come with you. I can help. I have my own food, and I can trap and hunt things. I'm actually quite good at hunting and tracking, so I can find things for us to eat. Plus, I know a lot about the wild edible plants that are in our state," Sam said, as he tried to catch his breath.

David shrugged his shoulders and looked to John and Laura, since this was mostly their trip. David had agreed to get them to where they needed to go, but David and Lisa were eventually going to make their way back to his family's place, so it didn't matter to him one way or another, as long as Sam could carry his own weight.

John furrowed his brow. He liked Sam and didn't have a problem with him coming, but he didn't really

STRIKE POINT: ADRIFT

know if Sam could fend for himself. John didn't want to be responsible for him if something happened.

"I don't mind if you come, but this could get dangerous," John said, hoping that maybe Sam would change his mind.

"No more dangerous than having a knife to my throat, and that's already happened to me. I want to come. Please?" Sam begged.

John nodded. "It could be quite a long trip. A lot of walking. And I have no idea what we'll find when we actually get there. But if you want to come, you're welcome to."

Sam smiled and they all began to head down the road towards the river.

CHAPTER 30

We did our best to stay along the banks of the river, but in several places it was just too wooded or rocky and we had to try to find a walkable path that wouldn't break an ankle.

We spent most of the day pushing to get as far as we could. We knew that this would take quite some time, especially because walking was going to take us a lot longer, and we all were still trying to recuperate from our run-in with Sayid.

David and I made sure to keep our wits about us as we traveled. The girls paired off and had quiet conversations among themselves to help them pass the time, and to keep their minds off of their aching feet.

The temperature had been decidedly warmer than we had wanted, but we were able to stay mostly under the trees and in the shade when we were walking, so that helped quite a bit.

Nightfall was coming and we needed to scout for

STRIKE POINT: ADRIFT

a place to camp that would give us access to the water, and would allow us to build a campfire without being detected.

We found a great spot that seemed to be surrounded by nothing but brush which could give us some privacy, but we worried that it would not provide enough shelter.

"If we take a bunch of branches and put them together around this area, we can pile up the outside with leaves to create more of a shelter and hide the fire," Sam suggested.

I was happy he'd felt eager to contribute, since most kids his age were just the opposite.

"That sounds great, but let's first do a sweep of the area to make sure that there isn't anyone already camping in the vicinity. Ladies, why don't you stay here and keep an eye on things? John and I will go around to make sure that there isn't anyone close by," David said.

"What about me? I can come with you and help scout the area," Sam asked.

David and I looked at each other and I saw no reason that Sam couldn't help. I nodded at him and he followed us out into the woods.

Since we had walked from the west, David went east and I went south. We sent Sam north towards the river. David and I went at least a half mile out, before zig-zagging our way back towards our own campsite.

David and I made our way back to the girls, having cleared our areas. Sam had yet to arrive, but we figured he was just being thorough.

"It looks pretty clear from where I was able to see. I think we'll be okay here for the night," David said and I agreed. It had already begun to get dark and we wanted to build a fire to be able to see.

I jumped when I felt the touch of something on my

shoulder. As I spun around, it was Sam who had easily sneaked up on me without me hearing him. Not only did that surprise me, but made me keenly aware that I had already let down my guard a little, and I needed to develop that skill even more.

"I think you need to come with me. There's something that you need to see," Sam said.

"What is it? What did you see?" Lisa asked Sam.

"I think it's some of the men from the house…um… from the camp. Some of the Jihadis," Sam said as his eyes lowered to the ground while he contemplated the significance of his words.

Laura and Lisa both stood up quickly. Their faces showed the fear that was solidly inside them.

David raised his hands. "Calm down, we don't know who they are yet. John and I will take care of it. You girls make sure your firearms are ready and stay low. If you want, go ahead and dig the fire pit and get it ready," David said.

Sam led us to the area where he'd seen the men. There were three of them and from the distance, I couldn't make out who they were, but I recognized the caps they were wearing. It was the same style of caps that the two Muslim men had been wearing when they'd circled our boat out on the water.

"It's them. I think it's the same two men that led us into the trap," I said to David who nodded in agreement.

"I'm supposed to give them the opportunity to surrender and be deported," David whispered.

I looked at him and raised my eyebrows. There was no way I was going to give them the opportunity to stay alive, not after what they'd done to us and to our wives, as well as anyone else that had crossed their paths.

"You may have had to take that seriously, but I don't.

STRIKE POINT: ADRIFT

I'm not in the military. I'm a civilian, remember? And if I need assistance, then your duty is to protect me, correct?" I asked David.

A sly grin grew across David's face as he nodded and raised an eyebrow. "Dispatch."

"Sam, would you please get back to the girls and just stay there armed with them? David and I will handle this. We want to do this quietly and without gunfire if we can. It would make me feel so much better if I knew you were there, protecting our wives," I asked him. I wanted to make sure that he wouldn't get killed if anything went south.

Sam nodded his head and slowly began to make his way back to where the girls were. David and I sat and waited until it got dark enough that their campfire would keep them from being able to see us easily, allowing us to use the darkness to our advantage.

We watched as one of the men decided to walk down towards the river. That gave us the opportunity to make our move. It would be much easier to take down two men instead of three.

David and I found a couple of trees that were wide enough to cover us with their shadows from the light of the campfire. David took a few rocks and began to throw them, so that it would distract the two Jihadis enough to want to investigate.

"Huh?" I heard one of them mumble something in Arabic.

The other one responded, but sounded as though he wasn't concerned. I watched as he took a swig of something from a bottle. It looked to be a wine bottle of some kind. If they'd been drinking, that would work in our favor.

The Jihadi that had noticed the sound, took his rifle

and began to investigate, walking into the woods, right where David was hiding. I watched silently as David pushed his body flat into the side of the tree, trying to become invisible.

David waited until the man went slightly past his position, then covered the guy's mouth as he took his knife and buried it in the man's back and up into his liver. I jumped out and startled the other man who raised up to hit me, but before he could, I dropped to my knees and buried my knife in his gut to the hilt.

It only took thirty seconds to take down both men. It surprised me how easily we'd been able to do it. We took both the bodies and dragged them into the wooded area to hide them.

We decided that we didn't want to wait for the third man to come back, so we quietly made our way down towards the river to find him. We found him sitting on a log, smoking a cigarette and watching the moonlight reflecting on the river.

I paused a moment, thinking about the situation. We didn't know who this man was and this was one of those situations where we probably should ask if he wanted the opportunity to be deported.

But since he had been associating with the two killers that we had just dispatched, we decided that it was too risky to leave him alive. David moved in and with one brisk movement, broke the guy's neck and he slumped over and fell off the log.

I finally let out the breath that I felt like I'd been holding all evening. The flood of adrenaline pulsing through me made my muscles feel weak.

I stood there and tried to gather myself as I began to see how once you find yourself in a position of being threatened, it becomes much easier to kill those who

STRIKE POINT: ADRIFT

threaten to hurt you or the ones you love.

I shook my head in disbelief at the fact that I had become a killer. But that's exactly what was happening. These people who had forced me into such horrid action, had turned me into something that I hated. My guilt and disgust was beginning to mess with my head.

There was a part of me that understood the need to protect my family against people that would do them harm, like these men. But I'd grown up believing that we weren't supposed to be killing people. That's just not something that most Americans did.

David came over and gave me a fist bump on the shoulder. He obviously had learned to deal with having to kill people, but I still was learning to process this new life.

We were just about to head back to camp when I spotted something floating off to the side of the river. I walked a little farther down the path and noticed that it was a boat.

Not just a boat…OUR boat. The one that had been taken from us earlier by these men.

"David, look," I said, pointing down river to the boat. I could just barely make it out in the moonlight, but he immediately recognized it.

"Holy shit! I hope it still has fuel," David said as he began to walk towards the boat.

I followed along and dug around in my pocket for my little flashlight. David stood between me and the river, so that when I turned on the light, it wouldn't be noticeable to anyone on the river. I ducked down and quickly turned on the light, shining it onto the gas gauge, then quickly turned it off.

"Why don't we wait until morning before trying to start it. It's kind of loud and it could be heard for quite some ways, so let's wait until morning," I suggested.

David agreed and we made our way back to camp.

"Did you take care of them?" Lisa asked.

"Sure did. We'll be fine tonight. But we have another surprise for you. For both of you," David said with a smile.

"I'm not sure I like surprises anymore. What did you find?" Laura asked, urging him to reveal his find. I agreed that it would be smarter to let them know what we'd found, in case they needed it for any reason.

"We found the boat. OUR boat. It looks like it still has a half tank of gas, but we didn't start it up to make sure it would still run. We were worried about being heard and didn't want it stolen overnight, so we'll go check on it in the morning," I said.

"You found the boat? Oh my goodness, I sure hope it still runs. I would love to be able to take the river, instead of having to walk all the way home," Laura stated.

"So would I. My feet are killing me and I have blisters that are not happy," Lisa said as she pulled off her socks to rub her blistered feet.

The rest of the night was uneventful. We started a small fire and ate, then took turns keeping a lookout while the others slept.

The next morning, we eagerly packed up our gear and made sure that we'd left our location as undetectable as possible. We made our way down to the river and everyone smiled to see that the boat was still in place. David and I eagerly jumped on board and I reached up to turn the key, when I realized that the key was missing.

"Oh crap. The key is missing," I said to David.

David rubbed his eyes. "It's probably on one of the men from last night. We'll need to go fetch it."

"I'll go. John, you can stay here with the ladies and

STRIKE POINT: ADRIFT

I'll go," Sam said.

David and I looked at each other and David shrugged. We weren't sure if Sam had already seen dead bodies that had been left for hours. I felt like Sam was trying to make a good impression on us and trying to become more of a man, even though he was still so young. But I had to let him learn about these things, and David was a very good teacher.

I nodded my head and Sam and David took off for where we had left the bodies from the night before. They returned a short time later, keys in hand and we were once again hopeful that we wouldn't have to walk all the way home.

David tossed me the keys and I pushed the right key into the slot. I eased it over and the engine rumbled to life, pushing the water from the back.

I smiled and looked over at the girls who were standing on the end of a log that had fallen into the water. I moved the boat over, so that it would be easier for everyone to get in without getting soaked. Once we were all on board, we slowly eased our way from the bank and headed into the open water of the river.

It was incredibly freeing, and the girls sat and relaxed a bit, knowing that we wouldn't have to walk the rest of the way. Sam and David each sat on opposite sides of the boat as I drove. They kept an eye on the shorelines, as well as anyone who happened to drive by. We only saw a few fishermen who kept themselves hidden underneath the low hanging trees.

We'd make sure to make eye contact and nod, but went on about our business. I wasn't about to let anyone take us again. Neither was David.

CHAPTER 31

I wanted nothing more than to open up the throttle and fly as fast as I could on that river. I felt that if we could hurry up and get there, that somehow we'd be out of the danger of being trapped on the water again.

David said that opening up the throttle would make the boat much louder and more noticeable, so it would probably be best to keep it at a steady pace that would instead, keep it at a lower volume.

"Sam, did you have any family back there?" Laura asked, standing up to stretch her legs and trying to make conversation.

Sam looked down to the water solemnly.

"Oh, I'm sorry. I shouldn't have asked..." Laura retracted, realizing too late that asking about family in this environment was probably the wrong question.

"It's okay, Laura," Sam reassured her. "I had a father. I didn't know my mother. She and dad divorced many years ago and she passed away from cancer two years

STRIKE POINT: ADRIFT

back. My dad owned the bank in town and she wasn't allowed to participate in my life."

Lisa furrowed her brow. The frown on her face spoke volumes.

"Why wouldn't your dad let you see your mother?" Lisa asked.

"There were two different stories. My dad said she was unfaithful, and she said it was him that cheated. I never knew who to believe until recently. Dad made sure mom wasn't allowed to see me and he had enough money to get the judges to do whatever he wanted. I didn't even know she'd died until six months afterwards."

Sam's eyes began to fill with tears as he looked out over the water. The rest of us just looked on in silence, letting him tell his story.

"When the power went out, I learned that my father had converted to Islam. I had always been raised Christian, but my dad gave me a Quran and made me read it. He wanted me to convert as well. I told him I didn't agree with what it said and that he was being manipulated. He got violent with me and told me that if I didn't convert, he'd have to kill me."

Laura recoiled in horror at Sam's words. The idea that a father would kill his own son because he wouldn't convert to Islam just wasn't something Americans could comprehend.

"So, did you lie about it to stay alive?" Lisa asked.

"Yes, I had to. If I hadn't, I'd be dead. I played the part of the good son, until I could figure out a way to leave and get free. But everyone was just barely surviving and I wasn't sure where I could go because I didn't know anyone. So I just stayed. Everything was going fine, until my dad told me I had to kill someone because they were Christian. That's when I knew he'd gone extreme. When

EMERSON HAWK

I refused, he turned me over to Sayid's men."

David shook his head. "Where is your father now? Is he still in town? That's something that's important for Knox to know."

"He's dead. I killed him," Sam replied.

There was an audible gasp from Laura.

"How? When?" I asked.

"When we all got back to town. I knew if he was left alive, he would only hurt more people. I couldn't allow that. Not after what he'd done to me."

Sam walked to the front of the boat and stood next to me, watching the river meet our bow. This poor young kid had already experienced things that he shouldn't have had to. I felt sorry for him. It also explained why he'd disappeared after we'd all got back into town.

"Once I got hydrated and got a little food, I waited by the back of the house until it got dark and I knew he'd be alone in the house. I let myself in with the hidden key that I'd placed there a few months back. Once inside, I held him at gunpoint, until I could get him secured to a chair in the living room. I took my time, but got all the answers I needed. I found out the truth about him and mom and that mom never did anything bad to him. That it was him who cheated. I told him that if he told me the truth, I would let him live. So he began to spill the beans about everything from our past," Sam said.

I was impressed with the calmness and strength that this kid had. I'm not sure at his age, if I'd have been able to do the same thing.

"He cried like a baby as he unloaded every evil thing he'd done to me and mom, and several other people in town. I didn't know just how bad he was until then. He made it easy for me. After he'd finished and I was done with him, I slit his throat and let him bleed to death on

STRIKE POINT: ADRIFT

his expensive rug. I'm sure if someone wants the house, they won't mind disposing of his body," Sam said, and he seemed to be at peace with his decision.

We all sat quietly, stunned at Sam's story. Sam turned around, and Lisa and Laura were both sitting there with tears rolling down their cheeks.

Sam smiled softly, "I'll be fine. I'm okay with what I had to do. He was an evil man. He was a banker."

David let out a little chuckle at the banker comment. I knew what he was thinking. It was the bankers that ran the world. They were the ones who had controlled the money and therefore, had controlled the politicians who'd brought this mess down on us.

It was those same politicians who hadn't listened when everyone had been yelling to harden the grid and find a way to bring manufacturers back to America, so we wouldn't be dependent on a foreign country to build the transformers we needed.

Laura and Lisa both got up and went over to hug Sam.

It was then that I realized that we had finally made it to our destination. The bridge at Chesterfield was just up ahead. We were almost home.

CHAPTER 32

There was a sense of relief that slowly came over the group as the bridge drew closer. The path that had brought them here had been long and full of death. John secretly hoped that the rest of the way would be much easier, but he knew better.

He knew that going into the city would likely be worse than anything they'd had to deal with yet. His goal at this point, was to get back to his niece and nephew's house to make sure that they were alive and hoped that they were still surviving.

"Look, there's the barge next to the port. If we pull up alongside it, we should be able to tie off without a problem," Sam said.

As they got closer, John lowered the throttle to try to keep the volume of noise down. John decided that instead of trying to dock in the open port area where they could be seen, he would first go past it so that they could survey the area, to see if there were any other people

STRIKE POINT: ADRIFT

around.

David agreed and the girls decided they would sit down lower in the boat, so that they wouldn't be seen while the men used the binoculars to scan the shoreline as they floated past.

It appeared that the dock area was deserted. So John found a spot right past the docking area to pull the boat in under some trees, and they were able to disembark and walk back through a small area of woods undetected.

When they got to the port area, they all stopped and listened to see if they could hear any kind of activity nearby. But it was dead quiet, which also made it creepy, considering they were near a city. The only sound that they could hear was of the river lapping up against the shore from the small wakes created by the wind.

"How do you want to handle this? Are you going to try to find some form of transportation or are you just going to walk back into town?" David asked John.

"Honestly, I hadn't thought that far ahead. I wasn't sure if we were going to make it this far. I would like to just walk along the highway all the way home, but that doesn't seem like the wisest decision. So, I think just staying near the roads that I'm familiar with will be the best course of action, trying to say hidden as much as possible. I know there will be areas that we'll have no choice but to be out in the open. We'll just have to take that chance," John replied.

"John, I know you want to check on your family and that is understandable. But this could get really dangerous. We have no idea what's waiting in the city for us. You don't even know if they're still alive. You know, you don't have to do this. If we cross the bridge and head west, we'll be at my family's property sooner, and you're more than welcome to stay there with us. After things clear up in a few months, and if we can find horses, we can come back," David said.

John looked out over the river, and then back over the highway that was littered with dead cars, before looking back down at his feet. He contemplated the decision to have come this far and decided that it made no sense to have made this trip and not try to get to his family. His niece and nephew had kids, and he was concerned that they hadn't survived, But he needed to be sure.

"I appreciate the offer and depending on how things play out here, I may just take you up on that. I'd love to meet the rest of your family and live in a place that's much safer. But I have to know if my niece and nephew are safe. If they're still alive or not," John replied.

David nodded his head, "Okay. Then let's figure out the best way to get there. How familiar are you with these roads?"

"Pretty familiar. Most of it is general directions that we can just take. When I would drive this route, I could just get on the highway all the way to 141 and then go south to Manchester, which is where they live. It's a straight shot from the highway. But, walking would be out of the way, so it's probably best to take the smaller roads through the communities and make our way across diagonally," John replied.

"How long do you think it will take us to get there?" Laura asked.

John shook his head. "I don't know. It all depends on what we run into between here and there. We may get lucky and everything is smooth going. But I wouldn't expect that."

They all checked their gear and began to walk down

STRIKE POINT: ADRIFT

the stretch of highway that connected to the bridge. They would need to exit and take some of the back roads, but for now, this was the best way to get started. They kept a watchful eye up ahead as they moved between the cars and the concrete walls. Those would actually protect them in case of gunfire, if there was any.

As they weaved their way through the cars that were dead, they could tell that most of them had been looted already. It was like some kind of auto graveyard, since the weather had already taken its toll on the cars. The cars that hadn't been looted, still had bodies in them that were of varying degrees of decay. The smell from the hot pavement and dead bodies made their stomachs wretch.

"We need to get off of this highway soon. I don't think I can handle the smell much longer," Laura said. Everyone nodded and they picked up the pace towards the next off ramp.

"I'm surprised that this bridge has not been at least partially cleared to use to travel back and forth," Lisa said.

"Yeah, I would've thought that people would have at least pushed the cars off to the side, so that horses or some other small transportation could be used," Laura said.

"Well, things are different in the city, I'm sure. Maybe that hasn't been a priority. Maybe people are just trying to find food and clean water," Sam said, trying to get in on the conversation.

David and John gave each other a knowing glance. Moving cars was the least of the concerns of a large metropolitan area. Just finding food and water, and finding ways to bury or burn dead bodies would probably have consumed the first ninety days of any disaster. Sickness and death would have been something that happened to many people in the first month. Most people only had a few days of food stored before they would have to go to a grocery store.

Once the store shelves were empty, there would be no deliveries and people would have starved to death.

"Let's exit off this next ramp and walk through the field. I would feel much better about this journey being off the road and being in an area where it's easier for us to hide," David said.

They made their way down to the streets of Chesterfield, trying to say hidden as much as possible in-between the buildings and houses. There was not a lot of activity that they could see, but when they did see someone, they tried to make sure that they kept their distance. They wanted to make sure that they didn't hurt anyone if it wasn't necessary, but they also knew better than to let their guard down as they traveled through town.

"Let's find a place to stop. If we can find a house that no one is in, then we can use that to rest," John suggested.

They made their way into a small neighborhood that had some houses that looked like they had been built in the 1970s. The houses all had the same designs, but were rotated so they probably had almost all identical floor plans. As they stood at the end of the street and looked down it, the group couldn't see anyone or hear any activity. It was eerie to be standing on a city street with no sound.

"So, what do you plan on doing? Just going to go door to door and knock?" David asked.

John looked at David and shook his head. "No, that's not a smart move. Maybe using a house is not the best option. Not unless we can secure it beforehand. How much longer do you all want to walk tonight? It's beginning to get late and we probably should try to find a place stay for the night."

"I'd like to stop now. If we can find a place that we can stay, then we could fix something to eat," Lisa said.

David led the group over to a small park-like area where they sat down on the grass, and tried to decide what the next course of action would be.

"I just don't think it's a good idea to go door to door. It's too risky because we don't know who's inside. It goes against all of my training to do things this way. We would be much better off to try to find a vacant building that we're pretty sure no one would stay in. It's less comfortable but it's safer to know that we wouldn't be shot," David explained.

Everyone agree with David that it would be better to try to find a place that they knew had been abandoned. Unfortunately, they were not in an area where there were a lot of old buildings. Chesterfield was not an area that had been around a really long time, and the area that they were in didn't have a lot of warehouses.

As they sat in the park to figure out what to do, Laura's attention was caught by a bright red ball that came bouncing out of one of the backyards.

Moments later, a young child came hobbling out from behind the bushes and followed the ball, laughing with a woman right behind him. The group watched in silence as they didn't want to startle the woman. The mother didn't notice them immediately, but when she looked over and saw everyone watching her, her face dropped and she grabbed her child and ran back towards her house.

"Wait, we won't hurt you. We just want to talk to

you," Laura said as she dropped her bag and ran after the woman.

"Laura, stop!" John yelled as he ran after Laura.

Laura had already made it to the back door of the house, and she was banging on the door.

"Please, we're just trying to find a place to stay for the night. We're not here to harm anyone. We just need a place to rest on our way to Manchester," Laura said through the door.

John arrived shortly thereafter and began to pull Laura away from the house. He knew it was unsafe to assume that just because it was a mother and a child, that it wasn't a dangerous situation. A mother protecting her child could be the most hazardous thing that there was on the planet.

"Go away. There's nothing here for you." A woman's voice yelled through the door.

"Okay. Fine, we're leaving, but do you know if any houses are empty on this street? We just need a place to sleep for the night. We're not looking to do anyone any harm," Laura yelled back to the voice behind the door.

John continued to try and pull Laura away from the house, but she resisted him, trying to continue her conversation with the woman in the house.

John was insistent that they leave and he continued to drag Laura through the backyard. Laura finally quit resisting and followed John out of the yard, but as they got to the tree line, they heard the back door of the house open.

A shotgun muzzle was sticking through the crack in the door, but was held down towards the ground. Laura felt that she was just making sure that they knew she was armed.

"Look, I just wanted to know if any houses were va-

STRIKE POINT: ADRIFT

cant, so we could sleep for the night. That's all," Laura said softly across the backyard. The door opened a little more and the woman stepped out.

"Do you have any food?" the woman asked. Laura looked at her and realized that she probably hadn't eaten much and probably had given most of it to her child.

"Yes, I have food. I can give you some of what I have, but I need to know where we can stay," Laura said, standing still at the back edge of the yard. The lady looked around and motioned to the house that was next to hers.

"That house has been empty since before the power went out. You're more than welcome to stay there. There's no one in it. The people that lived there were away on vacation when the EMP hit. I doubt they'll actually make it back from Bermuda," the lady said.

"Thank you, I'll be right back," Laura said as she and John went back to the rest of the group.

"What are you doing? You can't give away our food," John stated.

"I'm not giving her all of it, just a can of the peaches that I have. It's probably more than they've had all week, so I'm sure they'll be grateful," Laura said as she dug through her pack and pulled out a can of peaches and a can of tuna.

She knew that giving up this food might actually create a problem for her later, but it was worth it right now. They needed a place to stay and this was ideal because it was at the end of the block. If they needed to get out in a hurry, they could easily scatter through the trees.

"I'll be right back," Laura said as she walked back towards the house. John followed her with his rifle on the ready in case he needed to use it, but he knew it was probably going to be fine.

EMERSON HAWK

Laura went and sat the cans of food on the back porch step.

"Thank you," she said as she tapped softly on the door and walked back through the yard towards the group. She heard the back door open and the cans be picked up before it quickly slammed shut.

The group made their way into the house next door. David used his knife to pry open the door, and then used a kitchen chair to wedge under the door to keep it shut.

It was surprisingly clean, like someone had prepared it for guests. There were three bedrooms and a bathroom that had not been used. John went through the house and found the hot water heater. Tapping on it slightly, he grinned as he let everyone know they had plenty of clean water to drink.

Exhausted, they all ate and turned in for the night.

CHAPTER 33

The next morning, we made our way out of the house and down the street. We didn't see the woman and her child again.

In order to get to Manchester, we would need to cut through several areas that were well-to-do and only housed those super wealthy. Most of the properties were fenced with some kind of privacy or tall fence thing that would not allow us to cross the property, so we had to stick to the streets.

It was quickly noticed that the well-manicured lawns had been replaced by gardens of food. As we looked through the spiked fence, we could see plenty of vegetables. We all stopped and gazed across the large plot of food and wondered how this person was able to keep it from getting stolen. That's when we were approached by a heavily armed guard.

"You folks need to move on," the guard said.

We didn't delay and headed down the street as the

guard trailed behind us, making sure we kept going. But as we got closer to the property entrance, we noticed what appeared to be a group of people standing outside the gates, yelling and crying.

"So, what's the story here?" David asked the guard.

"These are the beggars that refuse to go plant their own gardens. We bring them out a few things occasionally, when we have extras. These are the remaining few leeches in our society who refused to go and work for themselves but instead, insist on someone giving them a handout," the guard said in disgust.

I got the distinct impression that these were probably just normal people who had no idea how to grow their own food.

"So where does all of this food go? The stuff that you guys keep?" I asked the guard.

"Whatever we don't put away, we take down to the market where it can be bartered with other gardeners and bought. There is nothing for free anymore. That system is done away with. You either produce or you die," the guard said curtly.

"The market? Where's the market?" Lisa asked.

"It's in Ballwin, in one of the parking lots of a major home store," he replied.

We decided to avoid the crowd of hungry beggars outside the front gates and moved around them to the other side, where we could see even more of the gardens that had been put in place.

It amazed me how large the amount of crops could be produced on some of the properties in the middle of a major metropolitan city. There really could've been plenty of food if everyone would have put in a garden and it would have helped many people to have survived.

If everyone would have grown some type of food,

STRIKE POINT: ADRIFT

there would have been more than enough for everyone. But people didn't think ahead and it took time to grow food. So, you still had to find ways to eat, in between starting your garden and harvesting.

It took us most of the day to make our way down to Manchester and to the neighborhood where my niece and nephew lived. Most of the houses were 1980s tract homes that all looked the same. We walked down the street and managed to see a few families that were still in their homes, but most of the houses appeared to be empty. When we got to their house, I stood on the front lawn and shook my head at what I saw.

Laura reached out and touched my arm. "Babe, I'm so sorry."

The house had been completely destroyed. All of the Windows had been broken out and the house had been completely looted. It looked like it had been abandoned for years, when it has only been a few months.

I walked inside the open front door and there were toys and furniture, broken and strewn all over the house. It stunk from rotten food that had been broken and left all over the floors. The bathrooms were full of shit where people had obviously been using them instead of using their own home. I felt my stomach lurch as I had to quickly exit the house from the overwhelming smell. As I ran out the back patio door, I immediately threw up from the emotional impact and the smell that now seemed to be following me out of house.

I looked around the backyard at the swing set that was broken and wondered what had happened to them. Where had they gone? I had no clue where to begin to look. My heart sank as I thought about them, and I desperately hoped that they were still alive, still trying to survive somewhere.

"Where do you think they would have gone?" David asked.

I shook my head. "There are so many cousins and friends. But if they were smart, they probably went to one of the in-laws out in the country."

"Is there any other place you want to look?" David asked.

"No. Let's just get to my place now," I replied.

CHAPTER 34

It took us several hours to get to the street that would lead us to our home. The closer we went towards the heart of the city, the more the bullets seemed to barely make it past our heads.

The closer that we got into the dense urban areas, the more we could tell that there was death all around us. The smell of decay and bodies was quite prevalent, and we noticed several piles of trash in vacant lots where we figured dead people were also tossed.

As we made our way through the neighborhood, the houses were in different states of destruction. Homes had been burned and some had been looted. Peoples' belongings were tossed all over the place.

"Why is it that people have to destroy property when things happen that are bad? I never understood this mentality. In times of hardship, it makes more sense to try to keep what you have in good condition, not tear it down," Laura said.

EMERSON HAWK

"I know what you mean! It always seems like on TV, anytime we would see some major event happen in a city, that people would go crazy and loot and destroy their own neighborhoods. It just never made sense to me either," Lisa replied.

It made my heart sad to see the difference from just a few months back. When we'd left, our neighborhood was clean and pristine. We weren't rich, but we were middle-class and everyone had taken care of their own property.

But now, it looked like some war torn battlefield. Most of the homes were either boarded up tight, or their windows were broken and the houses looted. Some of them were completely burned to the ground. Whatever had happened here, it'd been bad when it'd first started.

I was surprised at the lack of human activity in the area. It was almost deserted. As we made it to our street, I stood at the end of the block and looked down towards our house.

Our house was down at the dead end and most of the homes had been completely destroyed. I noticed the street had been littered with a bunch of paper flyers. Picking one up, I read the notice:

Food and water supplies to be given out down at the river. Come to the stadium to get your supplies.

That partially explained why so few people were around. If they had been telling people to go downtown to get food, then everyone had gone there and probably had stayed because that's where the food was. The only people who hadn't gone, would be the people who had prepared enough beforehand.

We made our way down the sidewalk and cautiously looked around as we walked, so that we would not startle someone if we came upon them, and accidentally

STRIKE POINT: ADRIFT

get shot.

When we finally made it to our house, we all stopped and just stared. Laura and I were stunned at what we saw. All of the windows were broken on the main floor. The front door was ripped off its hinges and lying in the yard.

"Why?" Laura cried out, and I understood her sentiment.

"I don't know. I mean I understand if someone's trying to find food. But, why so much destruction? It just boggles my mind," I replied.

David and Lisa tried to comfort us as best they could, but they knew that it probably was not going to be any better on the inside.

"John, you and I should scope out the inside before the girls come in. Sam, stay out here and keep an eye on things," David said.

I nodded my head, and we readied our weapons before heading inside. The inside was not much better. Everything had been destroyed. All of the glass was broken in the windows and all of the furniture had been demolished. It looked like someone had taken a knife to the sectional and just ripped it to shreds. The smell of urine was strong. It was like someone had come in and just pissed all over everything. It was disgusting.

I tried to hold back my emotions as I walked through my now mutilated house and surveyed the damage. There was little of anything left that was worth anything. We made our way down into the basement and any of the extra food had already been taken. I had expected that as soon as I'd seen the house broken into.

What I hadn't expected was the total damage that was done to everything in the house. It just made no sense to me.

EMERSON HAWK

After clearing the basement, we went back up to the second floor, to make sure that there was no one up there hiding in the closets or something. The upstairs was a mess, but it wasn't ravaged like the main floor had been.

We'd had a small safe in one of the closets that had been dragged out and pried open. It surprised me that it'd been opened at all, but apparently someone had been quite determined.

I'd had several thousand dollars in cash and Laura had saved up silver coins, in case cash wasn't worth anything during an event. It was all gone. Fortunately, the bed was not destroyed. In fact, it looked like it was the one thing that had not been touched.

I went into the guest bedroom and the computers were gone, but the furniture had been left alone.

"Well, if we have to stay here tonight, at least the beds are clean enough to sleep in," I said to David.

"How do you think Laura will react when she sees this?" David asked.

"Devastated. Just like I am. But there's nothing we can do about it," I replied as we made our way back outside.

"Babe, it's bad. I'm sorry. I had no idea this was what we'd be coming home to," I said as I motioned for her to come inside.

I watched her face as her emotions overwhelmed her. She began to cry as she saw how completely destroyed our home was. It was as if a tornado had come through and everything had been ripped to shreds.

I knew it would be hard for both of us to come to grips with what had happened. But I knew we would be able to move on and I knew we would survive. We had already survived so much already, that this was minimal compared to what other people may have experienced.

"How can people just do this? Why do people do this kind of thing? I understand if someone is breaking in to look for food or money for guns or something like that. But why destroy the furniture? And why does it smell like someone used the house as a urinal?" Laura said, the words just tumbling out in between sobs.

Lisa wrapped her arms around Laura's shoulders to try to console her.

"I know this must be so hard for you. I can't imagine having my entire home destroyed like this. But look at it this way, if there is a bright side, you weren't here when this happened. Who knows how things would have turned out if you would have been here when whoever did this came by," Lisa said, trying to give Laura some bit of hope.

Laura shook her head as she continued to walk through the broken glass and trash that had been piled up throughout the house.

"Well, I'm sure there's no food left here, so I suppose the only thing we can do is gather what few personal items we can find. How are we going to get windows replaced? There's no way that we can stay here," Laura asked, her mind running in so many different directions with all the work that would need to be done.

"We're not going to worry about that. We're not going to stay here. I made a mistake and I'm sorry. I thought we'd be able to come home and try to make it here, but I see now that that's not going to work," I said as I lowered my eyes to the ground.

I realized at that moment that staying in the city was not the best decision. Coming back to town was a bad idea. I had hoped that we could at least make sure my niece and nephew were okay, but I had no idea where they were and had no way of finding out where they had gone. All I could do now, was try to salvage what little bit we could while we were here, and see if David's offer was still open to come to his family's home.

David patted me on the shoulder and nodded for me to walk outside so we could talk. Sam was still out back, making sure that no one was approaching us as we headed out the back door.

As I looked out over the backyard, I realized that the privacy fence was still intact, so at least the backyard was somewhat private. I could feel the tears pricking at my eyes and I swallowed hard to make sure they stayed away. But it was hard to think about walking away from our home.

"You guys know that you can come with us. We can stay here tonight and head out at first light. We can gather what personal items that you want to bring with you and head back across the river to where my family's property is. I'm sure it's safe and it'll be a good place to start over," David said.

I nodded my head and rubbed my eyes, patting him on the shoulder.

"Yes, I think that's what we'll do. At least for now, we'll come with you and Lisa. We may decide to eventually head back to Ben's house but for now, that would be a good start for us. I'm truly grateful," I said.

Sam walked over and interrupted our conversation.

"So, are we staying here tonight?"

"We'll stay here for tonight, but we'll be heading back out first light. I'm sorry to have dragged you all the way here, Sam. But I appreciate you being here," I said with a halfhearted grin that I forced.

Sam smiled gently at me, understanding my current state of mind as best he could.

STRIKE POINT: ADRIFT

"Well, at least we'll have plenty of greens for tonight. Your entire yard is taken over by edible weeds, and I actually see a few tomatoes hidden under them. Those must be leftovers from your previous garden. And since the fence is so high, no one has bothered to check in between the weeds for the other plants," Sam said.

I smiled at him and nodded. He was a good kid and really was trying to do his part in this whole survival business. I appreciated what he was trying to do.

I made my way back inside and found Laura upstairs, sitting on our bed crying. I sat down next to her as she hugged me and buried her face in my neck, letting out sobs of pain as her emotions took over.

"I know, babe. I know it hurts, and I'm so sorry. Maybe it would have been better not to have known. But now that we're here, let's gather what we can and we'll go and start fresh in another place," I said.

She pulled away and nodded her head. I knew it was going to be a rough night.

CHAPTER 35

Lisa and David had taken it upon themselves to try to clean up the main floor area as best they could. They'd found an old broom and had swept up the trash and glass outside, so that at least they wouldn't be walking all over it.

Even with shoes on, a shard of glass going through someone's foot wasn't something anyone wanted to experience. So they managed to get the main floor area swept and any trash put outside. Just that little bit helped a lot. Removing the trash and glass made it feel less like someone had used it for a landfill.

The windows were all busted open, but David was able to find some nails and a hammer and began putting up boards he'd found from the dilapidated shed outside. He'd brought the front door inside and had nailed it into place, using a few longer boards to secure it. Having the door on, for some reason made it feel safer.

Unfortunately, the smell of the urine was not something that could be swept away. But Lisa had managed to find a small container of fabric refresher and began to spray it all over the house where the smell was coming from. It actually helped enough to make it tolerable for them to walk through the main floor of the house.

John and Laura made some progress upstairs as they found a few pictures remaining and decided to take a few pillowcases and create a couple of small bags of clothes to take them with them.

Laura finally stopped crying and took a deep breath, talking to herself and telling herself that this was a new beginning and to let the past go.

That's when Laura's face lit up and John looked at her quizzically.

"I just thought of something! I totally forgot about this before, but there may actually still be food here," Laura said to John.

John looked puzzled. "But, we already went through the entire house. If there'd been any food, it's been taken now," John said.

"Nope! There's a few places that unless you knew it was there, you probably wouldn't have looked," Laura replied.

Laura took off downstairs and John followed her, wondering what this revelation was all about.

It was an older house and in the dining room, were built-in china cabinets. The glass in the doors was all shattered, but the wood frame that held the cabinets against the walls was still intact. Laura smiled when she saw that the framing was still there.

"I need a Phillips screwdriver and a flat screwdriver, if we can find one," Laura said as everyone began to start the search for tools.

"I think I remember seeing some old tools downstairs when I was looking for the hammer and nails. I'll go check," David said and he took off into the basement.

A few moments later, he arrived with several tools that would work. Looking over the tools, Laura picked the ones that she thought would work best and got down on the floor, next to the china cabinet.

She took a Phillips head screwdriver and began to turn out a screw that had been holding one of the baseboards under the cabinet in place. Once she pulled it off, she carefully reached her hand in and pulled out a can of roast beef.

Laura's face beamed as she reached in and pulled out another can of roast chicken. As she kept reaching in, she kept pulling out food and handing it to the rest of the group as they all began to giggle at her discovery.

"How did you know this was here?" Lisa asked.

"Because I put it here. A few years ago, when I really thought the shit was going to hit the fan, I began to store food everywhere. But after a year or two of nothing happening, I kind of slowed down. So I would rotate the food, but I always meant to keep one area with at least a week's worth of food for David and I if we needed it. I knew that only a fire would take this out, but it was also a place for something else," Laura explained.

As she continued to pull out food, she also pulled out several spices and a box that when it was opened, revealed some cash, a black pepper box that had a dozen silver coins and some silver dimes and quarters, and a small handgun with ammunition.

John looked down at everything and looked at Laura in amusement. His wife was brilliant, and he really was proud of her at this moment.

"Why didn't you tell me?" John asked her.

"Because you thought I was crazy to begin with. You

STRIKE POINT: ADRIFT

thought I was overreacting to being prepared and after a while, I actually began to question what I was doing too. I felt that if I at least had a small stash somewhere, that only I knew of, that I could fall back on it. I should have told you, but I just forgot about it until now," Laura replied, sporting a cheesy grin.

That evening, they had a meal of stew with chicken, beef, rice and some of the greens from the neglected garden that Sam had found. It was delicious and hearty, and it filled them up which was needed since this had already been such a stressful trip.

As they all sat around the coffee table, that had been propped up with bricks from the backyard, they devoured the stew until everyone was almost too full.

As the darkness began to close in on the city, it began to take on an eerie quality. The gunshots seemed to be increasing as it got darker.

"We need to take shifts and keep an eye on the outside. Since the windows are broken out down here, I want to try to set up a few things. That way, if someone tries to come in a window, they'll be heard," David said.

Even with all of the windows boarded up, there would always be room for more security measures.

"I'll help," Lisa said as everyone began to gather things like cans and bottles and anything else that they could stack up underneath a window. The thought was that if there were things under the window that could fall and make noise, it would alert them to someone breaking in.

"Hey, is there still a ladder out back? Maybe over where the shed was?" Laura asked.

"I'll go check," Sam said as he made his way out the back door. At least the back door was still on its hinges.

A few moments later, Sam came back with a ladder

that had been hidden under a pile of wood.

"Sweet! I need it upstairs, and I'll need a flashlight or candle," Laura said.

"What are you doing?" John asked.

"You'll see," Laura said with a smile.

Laura took the ladder upstairs and placed it up under the attic access panel.

"Oohhh...whatcha got up there?" John asked.

"Oh, just some stuff and things," Laura giggled. "Just be ready for when I start handing it down."

Before he knew it, John was being handed plastic containers that had blankets, pillows and a cot, along with a couple of battery powered fans and lights.

"Where did all this come from?" John asked.

"Oh, just a few things I picked up here and there," Laura said, as she pulled the access door back over the hole and put the ladder into one of the other rooms.

"I figured, if David and Lisa want to, they can make a bed on the torn up couch. This will help make it comfortable. The cot is brand new and has never been used," Laura replied.

Between the quilts and blankets, it would make for a comfortable and clean place for them to relax.

Unfortunately, relaxing was going to be pretty difficult with all that was going on outside, but they were going to try and make the best of it.

CHAPTER 36

As I sat and looked out the second floor bedroom window, my mind was flooded with so many emotions that it was hard for me to come to grips with everything that had taken place. The last few months had been a whirlwind in a life that normally had been routine, and even somewhat mundane.

Our home that had been our refuge for so many years had been destroyed. This would be our last night here and it wasn't the safe place that I'd remembered.

"How are you?" Laura asked softly as she came and sat next to me on the bed.

"I'll be okay. It's just really hard, seeing this place like this. I had hoped that it would not have been this bad. I don't know why I thought maybe our place would have been untouched, I guess I was daydreaming, like most people in this country have been doing for years," I said.

Laura nodded. She knew what I meant. We all had

kept our heads buried in the sand for so long and never really had paid attention to what was going on outside of our own little worlds. We had become complacent and had never really thought about things other than our day-to-day routines.

But even if we had, I wasn't sure that there was anything we could have done anyway. As I thought about all of the things that were going on in the world, I felt very small and wondered if I could have made any kind of difference anyway. At least, I could have done more for our own protection, but I'm not sure that even that would have been enough.

The fact that we were out of town on vacation for a few days when this had happened, also made me think about how things could have been tragically different if we would have still been here when it happened. And if it had, would we still be alive? Would we have survived this long? Had we even have enough food supplies in our basement to stay alive for a few months? All of these things didn't matter now, but I still thought about them and wondered why we just didn't pay attention before.

"I'm looking forward to our new life together. At least there's some kind of hope, some kind of refuge that we may have at David's family's place," I said.

"I think it will be a good change for us. The city has never been welcoming to me. You know I've always wanted to live in the country anyway," Laura replied.

I nodded. I knew she had wanted to move out to the country for years. She'd begged me off and on whenever things would happen in the city that would irritate both of us.

We had experimented with chickens for a year or so in the city and never had any complaints, but the city always gave us grief even though everyone around us was

STRIKE POINT: ADRIFT

okay with it. It just seemed like they were looking for a reason to hassle us. But our neighbors rallied for us and squashed that. Then, there was the issue of crime and how it seemed to be increasing.

We were in one of those neighborhoods that bordered between a bad area and a very good area. It was an older neighborhood that'd had a blended community. Most everyone cared about their property and try to take care of it, but the property values were lower because the school system was in an area of town that was considered depressed. So we were able to have a nice home at a lower cost, but the cost of keeping it was having to be on the border of an area that also had a lot of crime.

Fortunately, we had never been victims of anything serious. Most of the neighbors on our block were gun toting and had no problems watching out for each other. That was the good thing about the neighborhood that we'd been in. Most people, whether they were Democrats or Republicans had still believed that firearms were our best defense against intruders.

We double checked everything with David and Lisa, who decided to take the first shift watching everything downstairs. After the windows and doors had been all boarded up, it felt safe enough for us to try to get some sleep.

"Laura and I are going to try to sleep for a while, so you guys come and get us when you're ready to crash. We'll head out at first light and make our way out of the city and hopefully, to a better place," I said to everyone.

David and Lisa nodded and they decided to play a few games of cards by candlelight when Laura and I decided to head to bed. Laura and I climbed into bed and I pulled her close to me. I wanted to snuggle up with her one last time in our own bed, before we left this place forever.

Even if the world went back to what it had been before, our house and all of the memories in it had been destroyed. I knew that I probably would never want to come back here again, and I was pretty sure Laura felt the same way.

I closed my eyes and tried to fall asleep, but the sounds of the house and the city were so different than what they'd been before. The windows upstairs had not been broken out, but they had to be left open in order for there to be some kind of breeze. There was no traffic noise, but the constant sound of gunshots off in the distance and at varying locations made it difficult to fall asleep.

As sad as I was to leave this place, and knowing I would be leaving it forever, I felt a glimmer of hope as I thought about the possibilities of what lay ahead. This world had changed so drastically in such a short period of time, that all I really wanted was someplace that felt safe and had some type of routine.

I knew we would eventually get there, but right now, we were still fighting in this new world.

CHAPTER 37

I watched as the sun began to shine through the kitchen window. The boards that had been put up allowed enough light to stream through, illuminating the dust that hung in the air as I walked through the house.

After Laura and I had gotten about five hours of sleep, we allowed David and Lisa to take the bed and we went back downstairs to keep watch, in case anyone tried to come in.

Sam had managed to get several hours of sleep in the guest bedroom which was great, so as everyone began to stir, we decided to try to put together something to eat for everyone.

Laura had managed to find some powdered scrambled eggs that she made along with some rice that was left over from the night before. We opened up our last can of ham and she mixed that into the eggs, and we had that over rice which was actually quite tasty. The combination of protein and carbohydrates was just what we would need to get a start on our day.

Once we finish gathering the few items that we'd decided to keep, we all headed out into the dawn and back towards the bridge that we had originally landed on.

I decided that we would take a similar route, since it'd seemed to be less crowded. We knew that it would take us probably six to seven hours of pushing to get back to the bridge at Chesterfield. We would camp overnight, and then make our way across the bridge and out towards Augusta where David's family's property was.

We had no idea how long that part would take, but we were ready to make the trip. We could stop at the river to fill up with water before heading across, making sure we were well hydrated, since we weren't sure what kind of water would be accessible later on.

The day was overcast and cloudy, like rain could come at any time. While I was grateful for the clouds, it seemed to make things much more humid. The humidity was almost unbearable, but we kept trudging on anyway, taking several breaks along the way just trying to keep ourselves from collapsing.

"I hate this humidity. I always get so chafed when I'm walking and it's this humid," Laura said, pulling at her clothing on different parts of her body.

"I agree. This is the kind of day I wish I would have brought shorts. But since I never know if I'll have to run and hide somewhere in thorny bushes…" Lisa said with a bit of a giggle. I knew she was trying to lighten the mood, but we were all just miserable. We all knew we had to keep moving and we chatted about how much we all missed air conditioning.

We continued our trek on the hard pavement and eventually got to some of the open fields in Chesterfield. The temperature had dropped significantly as soon as

STRIKE POINT: ADRIFT

we cleared the urban jungle and ventured out into the open fields.

I was always amazed at how concrete would radiate heat so much more, and just create a stifling bubble that would not release its grip in the hottest part of the summers. Being in the city was worse than being out in the country. Even at night, you could not get cool in the city. But in the country, you could actually sleep with your windows open if there was a breeze and be comfortable.

We decided to camp at a small clearing near the river that was surrounded by trees. It had been used previously, based on the burnt wood pile and ashes that remained.

Even though it was hot, we decided to start a small fire, just so that we could have some light when the sun went down completely. We decided to continue using the Dakota fire pit method, since we didn't want to give away our position. We weren't sure who else might be out here and we didn't want to risk being noticed.

Once it became dark, we all settled in for the night. I decided that I needed to take a bathroom break, so I grabbed my pistol and the shovel and took a little bit of a walk up the river, to find a private spot away from camp.

After I'd finished my business, I stood up and was buckling my pants when I noticed a small glow ahead of me. I decided to check it out, since it was so close to where we were camped.

I wanted to make sure that whoever it was, would not be able to see us. So before I approached, I looked back towards our camp and could barely see any kind of glow from our fire. It was just enough for me to get back because I knew which direction I had come from, but there wasn't the normal fire glow that a regular fire would have given off.

EMERSON HAWK

Looking forward again, I could see quite a large fire glow from someone up ahead. I carefully made my way through the trees, keeping myself hidden and using some of the stealth tactics that David had taught me. The closer I got, the more I realized it was just one person. I was surprised that one person would have created a fire this large. But maybe this person was just inexperienced. Or maybe just not afraid to be seen.

As I got closer, the person who had been sitting with his back to me stood up and I froze. I didn't want to be caught, even though I knew I could defend myself. The last thing I wanted to do was to have a fight on my hands.

But as this man stood upright, his physical form was familiar to me as he stood between the fire and myself. The outline of his figure was recognizable but I couldn't place him, until he walked around to the other side of the fire and faced my direction.

My heart sank into my stomach and I began to tremble slightly as I realized I was looking at Sayid. I decided that I needed David here to take care of this situation. We both had wanted him dead and it needed to happen now. This man was the antithesis of evil. I slowly began to walk backwards, paying attention to his face to make sure that he couldn't see me.

As soon as I got far enough away, I turned and double timed it back to our camp. Running in, I startled everyone.

"David, I need you to come with me right now. And bring your weapons," I said firmly.

"What? What is it?" Laura asked.

"Girls, please just trust me play. Stay here. We will return shortly and I'll explain then. Sam, stay here," I said, then looked back at David.

STRIKE POINT: ADRIFT

"We need to go now," I said with emphasis.

David didn't hesitate or question, for which I was grateful. He picked up his rifle and looked back at Lisa who nodded at him, then we both took off into the forest once again.

I stopped halfway between the two locations. "It's Sayid. He's here. We need to take care of this right now."

David's mouth dropped open. "No shit!" he whispered.

"It appears he's alone which is surprising to me, but apparently he started running and ended up here. Let's finish this," I said.

David and I made our way closer to the fire and I could see that his back was to me again as he sat on a stump.

"How do you want to handle this?" I whispered to David.

"My first reaction is to make it slow and painful. But, I just want to get it over with. I just want to make sure he's dead and can never hurt anyone else. I don't even care if he knows who it is. Let's just get this over with," David replied.

I knew what he'd meant, although there was a part of me that also wanted to make him suffer for everything that he had done to everyone that we knew. We just weren't like that, though. Instead of torturing him to death like we had fantasized about, we decided just to get it over with quickly and make sure he would not hurt anyone ever again.

"You're the stealth expert. You come from behind, and I'll go from the front. That way if he sees me, he won't be expecting you," I whispered.

David nodded and we began to make our approach. The adrenaline that was pouring through me was stronger than anything I had ever experienced. I had not really consciously planned someone's death before now. It was a strange feeling and one that I was not comfortable with. I didn't like thinking about killing someone. But killing someone that was so horrible, allowed me to justify my actions by ridding the world of evil.

I know that God says that we are not to kill someone, but I also know that God gave me the common sense to know the difference between right and wrong. And it was wrong to let this person live.

I moved around to the side, where I could approach Sayid from the front as David carefully crept from behind. David had his knife out and was ready as he grabbed Sayid around the neck and buried the knife into his back and up towards his heart. It was a move I had seen him use before, and it was quite effective.

As quickly as he'd buried his knife, he pulled it out and Sayid stood up momentarily and spun around, catching sight of both of us as we stood there facing him.

He began to say something in Arabic that neither of us understood as we watched him drop to his knees. He tried reaching around trying to hold the blood in his body, to keep it from gushing out of his wound.

I was satisfied that he would see David and I as his last sight before he died. He slumped forward onto his face as the blood began to pool around his body.

I decided that I would not take any chances and I reached down and grabbed his hair, using my knife to run across the jugular vein and slit his throat to make sure he bled out completely. I'm not sure exactly why I felt the need to do that, but I did it with no regrets.

David and I waited there until we knew for sure that this man would never live again. We decided that instead of burning his body, that we would just leave

STRIKE POINT: ADRIFT

it there for the animals to get. We put out his fire and cleaned ourselves up in silence. Regardless of the fact that this person was evil, neither one of us liked taking lives. It is against human nature to kill someone, unless they have harmed you and you fear they will continue to harm others.

After we stood and watched him bleed out, I felt a weight being lifted. Like we had done a small part in this new war.

We scavenged what we could from Sayid and made our way back to camp. I found myself shaking somewhat from all the adrenaline, my muscles aching from what felt like being in some kind of car accident. It was not a pleasant feeling. This world had changed me in so many ways that were not good.

At the same time, this new world had changed me into being stronger. It had turned me into a killer. Something I had never imagined myself being. It had changed me into a survivor. Something I was proud of being.

ALSO BY
EMERSON HAWK

Strike Point - Blackout (Book 1)
Strike Point - Caged (Book 2)

Grid Attack Cyber War The Trilogy.
Available in ebook, paperback an audio!

ABOUT THE AUTHOR

Thank you for your purchase!

Great reviews are the life blood of the modern day author. Without them, the hard work of the authors you love would disappear.

I would be grateful if you would leave a good review to let me and others know how you liked the story. You can also email me through my contact page on my website.

To see what other post-apocalyptic goodies Emerson Hawk has dreamed up for you to read, head on over to his website and sign up to be notified of new releases.

Website: www.emersonhawk.com
Twitter: @emersonhawk
Facebook: http://www.facebooks.com/emersonhawkwrites

Made in the USA
San Bernardino, CA
26 February 2017